The Body Lovers

MICKEY SPILLANE

G.K. Hall & Co. • Chivers Press
Thorndike, Maine USA   Bath, England

This Large Print edition is published by G.K. Hall & Co., USA
and by Chivers Press, England.

Published in 1999 in the U.S. by arrangement with Dutton Plume,
a division of Penguin Putnam Inc.

Published in 1999 in the U.K. by arrangement with Dutton Plume,
a division of Penguin Putnam Inc.

U.S. Softcover   0-7838-8540-7 (Paperback Series Edition)
U.K. Hardcover 0-7540-3727-4 (Chivers Large Print)
U.K. Softcover   0-7540-3728-2 (Camden Large Print)

The text of this Large Print edition is unabridged.
Other aspects of the book may vary from the original edition.

Set in 16 pt. Plantin by Minnie B. Raven.

Printed in the United States on permanent paper.

British Library Cataloguing in Publication Data available

Library of Congress Cataloging in Publication Data

Spillane, Mickey, 1918–
     The body lovers / Mickey Spillane.
       p. cm.
     ISBN 0-7838-8540-7 (lg. print : sc : alk. paper)
     1. Hammer, Mike (Fictitious character) — Fiction. 2. Private
investigators — United States — Fiction. 3. Large type books.
I. Title.
[PS3537.P652B64 1999]
813´.54—dc21
                                                              99-11732

This is for Bob Shiffer
who waited a long time

chapter one

I heard the screams through the thin mist of night and kicked the car to a stop at the curb. It wasn't that screams were new to the city, but they were out of place in this part of New York that was being gutted to make room for a new skyline. There was nothing but almost totally disemboweled buildings and piles of rubble for three blocks, every scrap of value long since carted away and only the junk wanted by nobody left remaining.

And there was a quality to the screams that was out of place too. There was total hysteria that only complete terror can induce and it was made by a child.

I grabbed the flashlight from the glove compartment and climbed out, picked a path through the mounds of refuse and ran into the shadows, getting closer to frenzied shrieks, not knowing what to expect. Anything could have happened there. A kid playing in those decayed and ruptured ruins could be trapped without having to do more than nudge a board or jar an already weakened wall. Aside from the occasional street lamps, there wasn't a light for blocks, and even the traffic detoured the section that handled the heavy equipment of the demolition crews.

But there wasn't any accident. He was just sitting there, a kid about eight in baggy jeans and a sweater, holding two hands clawlike against his face while his body wracked with his screaming. I reached him, shook him to get his attention, but it didn't do any good. I had seen the signs before. The kid was hysterical and in a state of shock, his entire body rigid with fear, his eyes like two great white marbles rolling in his head.

Then I saw what he was screaming about.

They had dropped the body behind a pile of cement blocks from a partly shattered wall, pulling a broken section of sheetrock over it to hide it from casual view. But there's nothing casual about a little kid who liked to play in junk and found himself stumbling over the mutilated body of what had been a redheaded woman. At one time she would have been beautiful, but death had erased all that.

I bundled the kid in my arms and got him back to the car. Along the way the breath had run out of him and the screaming became muffled in long, hard sobs. His hands clutched my arms like small talons and very slowly the knowledge that he was safe came into his eyes.

There was no use trying to question him. At this stage he was too likely to be incoherent. I started the car, made a U-turn and headed back toward the small trailer the construction company used for a watchman's shack.

From outside I could hear a radio playing and I shoved the door open. A stocky, balding guy

8

was bending over a coffeepot on the portable stove and turned around startled. "Hey . . ."

"You got a phone here?"

"Listen, mister . . ."

"Can it, buddy." I flipped my wallet out so he could see my New York State P.I. license and when he did he got a quick look at the .45 automatic in the shoulder sling. "You got trouble here. Where's the phone?"

He put the pot down shakily and pointed to a box built against the wall. "What's the beef? Look, if there's trouble . . ."

I waved him down and dialed Pat's office number downtown. When the desk sergeant answered I said, "This is Mike Hammer. Captain Chambers there?"

"Just a second, please."

Pat came on with, "Homicide, Captain Chambers."

"Mike, pal. I'm on the Leighton Construction site in the watchman's shack. You'd better get a crew and the M.E. down here in a hurry."

Almost seriously, Pat said, "Okay, who'd you kill now?"

"Quit being a comedian. There's a body all right. And get an ambulance here. I have a sick kid on my hands."

"Okay, you stay put. I'll get this put on the air and be there myself. Don't touch anything. Just let it be."

"Forget it. You tell the guys in the squad cars to look for my light. Somebody might still be

9

there . . . and there may have been more than one kid involved. I'll leave this one with the watchman. Maybe a doctor can get something out of him."

I hung up, went outside and brought the kid in and put him down on the cot the watchman used. The guy wanted to know what it was all about, but I cut him off, covered the kid up and told him to stay there until the police arrived. He didn't like it, but there wasn't anything else he could do. Then I got back in the car, drove up the road to where I had found the kid, parked up on the remains of the sidewalk so my headlights could probe the darkness of the buildings and hopped out.

Rather than silhouette myself against their glare, I skirted the beams, picking my way with the flash, the .45 in my hand on full cock. It was doubtful that anybody would stay around a body he had disposed of, but I didn't want to take the chance.

When I reached the sheetrock I stood still and listened. Across town the thin wail of sirens reached me, coming closer each second. But from the interior of the buildings there was nothing. Even a rat crossing the loose litter in there would have made a sound, but the silence had an eerie, dead essence to it.

I pointed the flash down and looked at the body beneath the hunk of sheetrock. She had been in her late twenties, but now time had ended for her. She lay there on her back, naked except for the remnants of a brilliant green negligee that was still belted around her waist. Her breasts were poised in some weird, rigid defiance, her long tapered legs coiled serpentine-like in the throes of death.

She hadn't died easily. The stark horror etched into the tight lines of her face showed that. Half-opened eyes had looked into some nameless terror before sight left them and her mouth was still frozen in a silent scream of pain.

I didn't have to move the body to know how it had happened. The snake-tail red welts that curled up around her rib cage and overlapped all the way down her thighs showed that. Dried clots of blood mottled the nylon of her negligee, stiffening it to boardlike hardness, some of it making the edges of her long hair like an old paintbrush. Tendrils of her life streaked her calves and the back of her neck, but the entire naked front of her was oddly untouched.

Somebody had strung her up and whipped her to death.

The flat of my hand touched the cold flesh of her stomach. Whoever it was had had plenty of time to get away. She had been there a good twenty-four hours.

Behind me the sirens screamed to a stop and the bright fingers of their spotlights swung in arcs, focused on me and held there. A voice yelled for me to stand still and a half-dozen shadowed figures began clambering over the rubble in my direction.

Pat was the second one to reach me and he told the uniformed cop holding his service .38 on me to put it away. Then I stepped back and watched the mopup operation go into action.

The Medical Examiner had come and gone, the morgue attendants had carted the body away to the autopsy room, the reporters and photogs had left the area strewn with burned-out flash bulbs that winked like dead eyes in the flood-lights the search team had set up and the kid had been taken to the hospital. Pat finished his instructions and nodded for me to follow him back to the car.

Not too far away was an all-night diner and we picked out an empty booth in the back corner and ordered coffee. Then Pat said, "Okay, Mike, let's have it."

"I gave it to you."

"Friend, I don't like that coincidence angle. I've found you on top of kills before."

I shrugged and took a sip of the coffee. "I'm not protecting a client, kid. Since noon I was out checking an accident report for Krauss-Tillman on the new Capeheart Building. That's five blocks north of the spot where I found the kid."

"I know where it is."

"So check on me."

"Hell, if I didn't know better, I would. Just don't make this any of your business."

"Why should I?"

"Because you have a big nose. That's what you

told me at dinner last night. I'll be damn glad when you marry Velda and she nails your shoes down."

"Thanks a bunch," I grinned at him.

He nodded, picked up his coffee and tasted it, not answering.

Pat and I had been friends too long. I could read him too well. He could say as much without saying a word as he could in a conversation. The years since we first met had hardly left a trace on him; he still resembled a trim business executive more than he did a cop . . . until you got to his eyes. Then you saw that strange quality that was a part of all professional cops, that of having seen trouble and violence so long, fought it step for step, that their expression was like seeing instant history, past, present and future.

I said, "What's on your mind, Pat?"

And he knew me too. I was the same as he was. Our fields were different, but allied nevertheless. We had been together on too many different occasions and we had stood over too many dead bodies together for him not to get my implication.

"It was that thing she wore," he told me.

"Oh?"

"Remember that blonde we fished out of the river last month . . . a schoolteacher from Nebraska?"

"Vaguely. It was in the papers. What about her?"

"She wore a gimmicky robe just like that one, only it was black."

13

I waited and he looked at me across the coffeecups. "It's on the books tentatively as a suicide, but our current M.E. has a strange hobby, the study of chemically induced death. He thinks she was poisoned."

"He thinks? Didn't he perform an autopsy?"

"Certainly, but she had been in the water a week and there was no positive trace of what he thought could have caused it."

"Then what shook him?"

"A peculiarity in the gum structure common to death from that cause. He couldn't pin it down because of time submerged in water polluted from a chemical treatment unit that was located nearby. He wanted to do some exhaustive tests, but the possibility was so remote and the evidence so inconclusive that we had to release the body to the girl's parents, who later had it cremated."

"Something else is bugging you," I reminded him.

He had another pull at the coffee and set the cup down. "If the M.E. was right, there's another factor involved. The poison he suggested was a slow-acting one that brought death about very gradually and very painfully. It is used by certain savage tribes in South America as a punishment to those members who have committed what they consider to be a serious offense against their taboos."

"Torture?"

"Exactly." He hesitated a second, then added,

"I got a funny feeling about this. I don't like your being involved."

"Come on, Pat, where the hell would I come in? I dumped it in your lap and that's as far as I go."

"Good. Keep it like that. You know how the papers handle anything you're involved in. It's a field day for them. You always did make good copy."

"You worrying about the new administration?"

"Brother!" Pat exploded. "The way our hands are tied between politics and the sudden leniency of the courts it's like trying to walk through a mine field without a detector."

I threw a buck down on the table and reached for my hat. "Don't worry about me," I said. "Let me know how it turns out."

Pat nodded and said, "Sure." But there wasn't any conviction in his voice at all.

The morning was colored a New York gray, damp with river fog that held in suspension the powdered grime and acid grit the city seemed to exhale with its breathing process. It came from deep inside as its belly rumbled with early life, and from the open wounds on its surface where antlike people rebuilt its surface. Everyone seemed oblivious to the noise, never distinguishing between the pain sounds and the pleasure sounds. They simply followed a pattern, their own feet wearing ruts that grew deeper and deeper until there was no way they could get out of the trap they had laid for themselves. Sometimes I wondered just who was the master and who was the parasite. From the window of the office I looked down and all I could see was a sleeping animal covered with ticks he could ignore until one bit too deep, then he would awaken to scratch.

Behind me the door opened and the faint, tingling scent of Black Satin idled past on the draft from the hall. I turned around and said, "Hi, kitten."

Velda gave me that intimate wink that meant nothing had changed and dropped the mail on the desk. She was always a surprise to me. My big girl. My big, beautiful, luscious doll. Crazy titian hair that rolled in a pageboy and styles be damned. Clothes couldn't hide her because she was too much woman, wide shouldered and breasted firm and high, hollow and muscular in the stomach and flanked with beautiful dancer's legs that seemed to move to unheard music. She was deadly, too. The tailored suit she wore under the coat hid a hammerless Browning and her wallet had a ticket from the same agency that issued mine.

Pretty, I thought, and I was such a damn slob. We never should have let it go this long. I had tasted her before, felt that wild mouth on my own and fallen into the deep brown of her eyes.

Crazy world, but she was ready to play the game out as long as I had to.

16

"See the papers?" she asked me.

"Not yet."

"You did real well. I can't leave you alone for a minute, can I?"

I picked up the tabloid and shook it out. I was there, all right. Page one. The department had held back the details, but it was a big spread anyway. The inside story gave the account of what had happened in general, me hearing the kid and finding the body, but no mention was made of the way the girl had died. Most of the yarn concerned the kid who had been playing on the site and accidentally came across the corpse when he lifted the sheetrock.

As yet no identification had been made of the woman and no witnesses to the disposal of her body had been located, but my accidentally stumbling on the scene was played up and some of my history rehashed for the public benefit. The writer must have been somebody I bucked once, because the intimation was that it involved me personally. Coincidence was something not acceptable to him. At least, not with my background.

I tossed the paper down and pulled a chair up with my foot. "Here we go again."

Velda shrugged off her coat and hung it up. I recited the incident all over again and let her digest it. When I finished she said, "Maybe it'll be good for business."

"Nuts."

"Then stop worrying about it."

"I'm not."

17

She turned and smiled, the even white edges of her teeth showing beneath that full, rich mouth. "No?"

"Come on, sugar."

"Get it out of your system. At least call Pat and find out what it's about."

"Dames," I said, and picked up the phone.

His hello was cool and he didn't repeat my name, so I knew he had company in the office. He said, "Just a minute," and I heard him get up, walk to the filing cabinet and slide a drawer open.

"What is it, Mike?"

"Just my curiosity. You get anything on that kill?"

"No I.D. yet. We're still checking the prints."

"Any dental work?"

"Hell, she didn't even have a filling in her mouth. She looked like a showgirl type so she might have a police registration someplace. You talk to any reporters yet?"

"I've been ducking them. They'll probably dig me out here, but there's nothing I can tell them you don't know. What's the matter, you don't sound happy."

"Mitch Temple from *The News* spotted the similarity in those flimsy robes that were on the bodies. He got lucky in checking out the labels and beat us to the punch. They were purchased in different spots — those shops that specialize in erotic clothes for dames. No tieup, but enough to hang a story on."

"So what can he say?"

"Enough to stir up some of these sex-happy nuts we have running loose around here. You know what happens when that kind of stuff hits the papers."

"Anything I can do?"

"Yeah . . . if you know Mitch well enough, tell him to lay off."

I grinned into the phone. "Well now, this can be a fun afternoon."

Pat grunted and said, "I suggested you *speak* to him, buddy."

"Sure, buddy. The point is loud and clear. When do you want my official statement?"

"Right now if you can get the lead out."

When I hung up I gave Velda the rundown and reached for my hat. She gave me that funny quizzical look and said, "Mike . . ."

"Yeah?"

"Did Pat notice the color relationship of those negligees?"

"Like what?"

"Black on a blonde and green on a redhead."

"He didn't mention it."

"They aren't exactly conservative. They're show-off things to stimulate the male."

"Pat thinks the last one was a showgirl."

"The other was a schoolteacher though."

"You're thinking funny thoughts, girl," I said.

"Maybe you ought to think about it too," she told me.

chapter two

My reception at headquarters wasn't exactly cordial. I gave a detailed statement to a police stenographer in Pat's office, but when he got done with the routine interrogation the new assistant D.A. took it from there, trying to sweat out some angle that connected me to the case. Luckily, Pat deliberately checked out my movements and corroborated them ahead of time, getting both of us off the hook, but not without getting the eager-beaver assistant D.A. red in the face. He gave up in disgust and stamped out of the office after telling me to stay in town.

"He must have read that in a book somewhere," I told Pat.

"Don't mind him. The front office gets spooked when sensational cases hit the papers in an election year."

"Don't kid with me, Pat. It smells like they're setting you up to be the patsy if something goes sour."

"You know how they're shaking up the department. Too many of the good ones already retired out in disgust."

"Don't let those political slobs ride you."

"I'm a paid employee, buddy."

I grinned at him. "Well, I'm not, and I got a big mouth. Outside a dozen reporters are waiting for me to show and I can do a little sounding off when I get rubbed wrong."

"Knock it off."

"Hell, no trouble."

"Forget it. You get to see Mitch Temple?"

"Not yet."

"Do that much and you'll do me a favor. That's all I ask. The rest we can handle just fine right here."

"I told you before I'm not in this."

"Tell it to the boys waiting outside." He got up and waved to the door. "Let's go. Your public awaits."

Pat sweated out the interview with me, watched me stand for pictures and nodded with approval when I parried the questions. For a change I didn't have to dodge and they knew it was because my story was a straight one. A couple wanted my opinion on the kill, but I shrugged it off. So far it was only Mitch Temple who had tried to tie in the earlier murder with the redhead, so there wasn't anything from that direction. If there was a tieup, Pat would find it. Right now it was only guesswork.

When they finished with me we went down to the coffee urn and drew a couple of cups. "You did pretty well back there."

"Nothing to tell them."

"Thanks for not guessing. Maybe I have something to tell you."

"Maybe I'd just as soon not know."

"Yeah," Pat said sourly. "So far there's no definite connection with those negligees. If the first one was a suicide, it's common enough. More than half who do the dutch act go out naked or partially dressed, though damned if I know why."

"You said *if*, Pat."

"Our little M.E. friend pursued his hobby further than I thought. Before they carted the corpse off he took tissue samples for further study. He won't commit himself positively, but he seems satisfied that his diagnosis was correct. As far as he's concerned, that first dame was poisoned, slowly and painfully."

"What can you do about it?"

"Nothing. There's no body to exhume and no way of proving those tissue samples came from the original corpse. Given a few more days and there won't be any trace of the chemical that was administered. It's deteriorated."

"And the other one?"

"A whip that left pretty definite imprints on the flesh. They match specialty items shipped from Australia for a few circus and stage acts."

"Trace the buyers?"

Pat nodded. "The regulars buy them in dozen lots. Straight people. The trouble is, the import house plants them around in all sorts of places . . . even to advertising them in those fetish magazines. We checked their orders and they've sold hundreds by mail alone. It would be damn near impossible to trace one back."

"That leaves her prints."

"And her pictures. The photo lab did a pretty good job of reconstructing her as she must have looked." He held out a four-by-five glossy and I scanned it closely. "Faces like that get remembered," he told me. "She was quite a beauty."

"Can I keep this?"

"Be my guest. It'll be in the paper anyway."

"Good deal. I'll call you after I see Temple."

"Think it'll do any good?"

I let out a short laugh. "I know a few things he wouldn't want to get around."

At twelve-thirty I met Mitch Temple at the Blue Ribbon Restaurant on Forty-fourth Street. He had been an old-line reporter who finally made it with a syndicated column and success seemed to have made him more cynical than ever.

I didn't have to tell him what I was there for. He had laced the facts together as soon as I had called him, and when we had a drink and put our order in he said, "How come you're the errand boy, Mike?"

"Because I might be able to squeeze harder."

He gave me a lopsided grin. "Don't hound me about that party on the yacht. You've used that twice already."

"Then how about the story you never wrote about Lucy Delacort? That house she ran . . ."

"How did you know about that?"

23

"I got friends in strange places," I told him. "Old Lucy really went for you, didn't she? In fact . . ."

"Okay, enough, enough. What do you want?"

"Pat says to lay off the negligee angle in those two deaths."

His face became strangely alert. "I was right," he said softly, "wasn't I?"

"Got me, Mitch. Pat doesn't want to stir in a sex angle, that's all. It gives the wrong people ideas. Give him a few days to work it out and you can do what you please. Can do?"

"That louses up a lot of legwork. I busted my tail tracking down those labels."

"How much did you get?"

Mitch shrugged. "The probable sales outlets. The clerks couldn't give me anything definite because they were hot items. You know, out-of-towners getting something sexy for the wife back home, servicemen making points with a broad, buying exotic goodies in the big city . . . dames trying to stir a little life into the old man with a little nylon lust."

"That's all?"

"I couldn't get a description to save my tail. Except for a couple of limp characters who took sizes they could wear themselves. Apparently they were regular customers. I could run them down all right, but I don't think it would do any good. Maybe you have an idea."

"Fresh out," I said. "Velda mentioned the color combinations, green with the redhead and

24

black with the blonde if it means anything."

"Hell, they were the fastest selling numbers. They didn't even have a pink or a white in stock. Nobody's modest these days." Mitch leaned back in his chair. "Maybe you'd better tell Pat I'm still working on it."

"So's he."

"I'm surprised nobody else made the connection. It isn't a big one, but it's a connection."

"Probably because that schoolteacher was a suicide."

"Now I'm beginning to wonder about that too," Mitch growled.

"So's Pat, but he's seen other suicides go out in their scantiest. Seems to be a common practice."

"Yeah, I know. She could have had a coat on before she hit the river. Nobody would have noticed her then. If she dropped it any one of that crowd along the docks would have picked it up and hocked it for a drink without thinking about it."

"What'll I tell Pat?"

"I'll play along for a week. Meanwhile, I'll still try to get an angle on those gowns." He looked across his glass at me. "Now what about you, Mike? You've always made interesting copy. Where do you stand?"

"Out of it. I'm a working stiff."

"You're not even curious?"

"Sure," I grinned, "but I'll read about it in *The News*."

After lunch I walked to Broadway with Mitch,

turned north and headed back to the office. The morning damp had turned into a drizzle that slicked the streets and turned the sidewalks into a booby trap of umbrella ribs. The papers on the newsstands were still carrying front-page stories of the death of the redhead and the afternoon edition of one had a nice picture of me alongside the body shot of the corpse and one of the kid. I bought three different papers, stuffed them in my raincoat pocket and turned in at the Hackard Building.

Velda had left a note saying she was going to do some shopping and would be back later. Meanwhile, I was to call the Krauss-Tillman office. I dialed Walt Hanley at K-T, got his instructions on another job, hung up and added a postscript to Velda's note saying that I'd be out of the city for a few days and to cancel our supper date.

She was going to be sore about that last part. It was her birthday. But I was lucky. I had forgotten to buy her a present anyway.

The few days were a week long and I stopped by the office at a quarter to five. Velda sat there typing and didn't even look up until she had finished the page. "Happy birthday," I said.

"Thanks," she said sarcastically.

I grinned and tossed down the package I had picked up ten minutes ago. Then she couldn't hold the mad any longer and ripped the paper off it. The pearls glinted a milky white in the light and she let out a little squeal of pleasure. All she could say was, "They real?"

"They'd better be."

"Come here, you."

I leaned over and sipped at the rich softness of her mouth and felt that same surge of warmth that came over me whenever she did those woman-things to me.

I pushed her away and took a deep breath. "Better quit while you're ahead."

"But I thought you were winning."

"You were drowning me, kitten."

"Just wait till later."

"Stop talking like that, will you?" I said. "I've been stuck in the bushes a week until I'm ready to pop."

"So I'll pop you."

I rumpled her hair and perched on the edge of the desk. She had my mail stacked up in three piles, circulars, business and personal, and I riffled through them. "Anything important?"

"Haven't you been reading the papers?"

"Kid, where I've been there wasn't anything but hills and rocks and trees."

"They identified the redhead that was killed."

"Who was she?"

"Maxine Delaney. She was a stripper on the West Coast for a while, was picked up twice in a suspected call-girl operation, but released for lack of evidence or complaints by parties involved. She was last heard of in Chicago where she was registered with a model agency and did a few nudies for a photographer there."

"I meet the nicest people, don't I? Any mail?"

"Nothing special. You got a package there from a pen pal, though."

In the personal pile was a flat, six-inch square package with a box number address and a postmark from that famous city on the Hudson that harbors New York's more notorious ex-citizens. I tore it open and took the lid off the box inside.

A stenciled letter informed me that the enclosed was made by a prison inmate and any voluntary contribution I cared to make would go in the recreational fund. The enclosed was a neat black handmade leather wallet and tooled on the front in an elaborate scroll was MICHAEL HAMMER, INSURANCE ADJUSTER. And it was such a nice piece of work too.

I tossed it in front of Velda. "How about that?"

"Your reputation has gone to the dogs." She looked up, read the letter and added, "They have a complaint department?"

"Send five bucks. Maybe it's deductible." I dropped the wallet in my pocket and slid off the desk. "Let's have some supper."

"Okay, insurance adjuster."

We were going out the door when the phone rang. I wanted to let it ring, but Velda was too much a secretary for that. She answered it and handed it to me. "It's Pat."

"Hi, buddy," I said.

I couldn't quite pin down his tone of voice. "Mike . . . when did you see Mitch Temple last?"

"A week ago. Why?"

"Not since?"

"Nope."

"He give you a hard time or anything?"

"Hell no," I told him. "I gave you all the poop on that deal."

"Then tell me this . . . you got a straight alibi for, say . . . twenty-four hours ago?"

"Buddy, I can have my time and places verified by three witnesses for the past seven days to this minute. Now what gives?"

"Somebody bumped Temple in his own apartment, one knife thrust through the aorta, and he died all over his fancy oriental rug."

"Who found him?"

"A girl friend who had a key to his apartment. She managed to call us before she went to pieces. Get up here. I want to talk to you."

I hung up and looked at Velda, knowing my face was pulled tight. "Trouble?" she asked me.

"Yeah. Somebody killed Mitch Temple."

She knew what I was thinking. "He was poking around on that girl's murder, wasn't he?"

I nodded.

"Then what does Pat want with you?"

"Probably every detail of our last conversation. Come on, let's go."

Mitch Temple had an apartment in a new building on the east side, a lavish place occupied by the wealthy or famous, and the uniformed doorman wasn't used to seeing squad cars and police officers parked outside the ornate doorway.

29

The cop on duty recognized me, passed me through and we took the elevator up to the sixth floor. Two apartments opened off the small lobby, one apparently belonging to an absent tenant, the other wide open, the cops inside busy with routine work.

Pat waved us in and we skirted the stain on the floor near the door and followed him across the room to where the body lay. The lab team wound up their work and stood to one side talking base-ball. I said, "Mind?"

"Go ahead," Pat told me.

I knelt by the body and took a look at it. Mitch Temple lay sprawled on his side in a pool of blood, sightless eyes glazed with death. One hand was still stretched out, clawing at his suitcoat he had jerked off the chair back, his fingers clutching the white linen handkerchief he always wore in his breast pocket. I stood up and looked at the trail of blood from the door to the hole in his chest. It was a good twenty feet long.

"What do you make of it, Pat?"

"Looks like he opened the door to answer the bell, took a direct stab from an eight-inch knife blade and staggered back. Whoever killed him just closed the door and left."

"A wound like that usually drops a man."

"Most of the time."

"What was he after in his coat?"

"Something to stop the flow of blood is my guess. Nothing seems to have been touched. I'm surprised he lived long enough to get that far. So

30

was the Medical Examiner. He fell twice getting to his coat and crawled the last few feet."

"Nobody comes into these apartments without being announced downstairs first," I reminded him.

Pat gave me a disgusted look. "Come on, we haven't pinpointed the time of death yet, but a pro could manage it at the right time. These places are far from foolproof. We're checking out the tenants and anybody else who was here, but I'm not laying any bets we'll come up with something. The type who live here don't want to be involved in any way. They don't even know their next-door neighbors."

"That's New York," I said.

"Now how about you." It was a statement, not a question.

I looked at him and shook my head. "Count me out. I haven't had contact with him since I saw him last. I told you what he said . . . he'd lay off his story for a week, but meanwhile he'd keep on working that negligee angle. Think he found something? He had a lot of sources."

Pat shrugged. "Neither his paper nor his secretary had any record of his movements. She said he was gone a lot, but he turned out his column regularly. We're backtracking the items he reported in case it ties in with one of them."

"How about that series he did on the Mafia last month?"

"They're too smart to buck the press. It wouldn't stop anything and throw too much light on them. They want anonymity, not publicity. This is something else."

"Those damn negligees?"

"It's a possible. I hoped you'd come up with something."

I reached in my pocket for my cigarettes and got the wallet instead. "Hell, I'm only an insurance adjuster," I grinned. "It says so right here." I tossed the wallet to Velda. "Here, you can have it." She caught it, and like all women, dropped it in her pocketbook. "Sorry, Pat. I can't give you a damn thing. That is, unless the police department wants to employ me."

"Yeah," he grunted. "I can picture that. Well, you might as well get out of here before the press arrives. They'll blow this one sky high as it is and I don't want them getting cute followup angles involving you."

"Count me out, old buddy."

"If you hear of anything, let me know."

"Sure will."

"There's a side entrance. Take that out."

We started for the door and I turned around as I reached it. "Mind letting me know how things shape up?"

Pat's mouth twitched into a smile. "Okay, nosy."

Supper was a steak in Velda's apartment, a homey little arrangement she set up deliberately, a perfect man trap if there was one. She wore a quilted housecoat of deep blue, belted loosely enough so that when she walked each step ex-

32

posed a satin length of calf and thigh, provocatively out of reach as she passed by. Sitting opposite me, the lapels stretched over the deep swell of her breasts, and with the gentlest motion of her shoulders, fell apart so I could be taunted by her loveliness.

I finally pushed the plate away, the steak finished, but untasted. She poured the coffee, grinned and said, "See what you're missing?"

"You're a nut." I fished my cigarettes out and stuck one in my mouth. "Light me, will you?"

Velda reached for her pocketbook, dumped some of the stuff out until she found matches and lit my butt. When she was putting the things back she paused with the wallet in her hand and said, "Why would an inmate send you that?"

"You saw the letter. It's part of their rehabilitation program."

"No, I don't mean that. If they're sent to well-known people, certainly they wouldn't mistake their occupation. Especially not yours. It's too bad there's no name of the maker."

"Let's see that." I took the wallet and flipped it open. It was of standard design with card pockets, an identification window and a section for bills. I felt in all the compartments, but nothing was there. "Empty," I told her. "Besides, these things would be checked to make sure nobody was sending messages outside. It could be a cute gimmick."

"Maybe it has a secret compartment," she laughed.

33

But I didn't laugh. I stared at the wallet a long moment, then felt around the folded edges until I found it, a cleverly contrived secret pocket that cursory examination would never uncover.

That's where the note was.

It was written in pencil, printed in tiny caps on toilet paper. I read it twice to make sure of what I had, digesting every word. *Dear Mike, Heard about that redhead on the radio. My sister knew her and the Poston dame. Didn't think much about it when the Poston kid died, but this one bothers me. I ain't heard from Greta in four months. You find her and make her write and I'll pay you when I get out.* It was signed, *Harry Service.*

Velda took the note from my fingers and read it over, frowning. "Poston," she said softly. "Helen Poston. That was the schoolteacher who committed suicide."

"That's the one."

"But this Harry Service . . . wasn't he the one . . . ?"

"Yeah, I got him sent up."

"Why would he write to you?"

"Maybe he doesn't hold a grudge. Besides, he's not the type to confide in cops. He wouldn't give them the sweat off his butt."

"What're you going to do about it, Mike?"

"Damn it," I said, "what can I do?"

"Let Pat have it."

"Great. Then word gets around I'm a first-class fink. Harry went to all that trouble to get this to me. The insurance adjuster bit was supposed to tip me and I'm thick-skulled about it."

Velda handed the slip back to me. "You don't owe this Service any favors."

"Not in the ordinary sense. Even though I nailed him in that robbery and he tried to kill me, he still figures I'm square enough to deal with." I glanced at the note again. "It's a crazy request."

"What you're thinking is even crazier."

"A wild kind of a client."

She gave a little shrug of resignation. "Pat doesn't want you playing with this thing. You're only asking for trouble."

"Hell, all I'm doing is locating a missing person."

"You're rationalizing," she said. "But go ahead, you'll do it anyway. Only don't start tonight, okay?"

"Okay."

"Okay then," she repeated with an impish grin and came into my arms. On the way she tugged at the belt and I felt wild little fingers crawl up my spine.

chapter three

The file on Harry Service listed his sister Greta as next-of-kin. He had taken a seven-to-fifteen-year fall on that armed robbery rap a year and a half ago and at that time her address was listed as being in Greenwich Village. I never remembered her being at the trial, but when I went through the back issues of the paper there was one photo of the back of a woman in a dark coat squeezing Harry's arm after he was sentenced.

It was a little after two when Hy Gardner got to his office. He waved me into a chair and sat down behind his typewriter. "What's on your mind, Mike?"

"The Service trial."

"You did him a favor slamming him in the cooler. That way he won't make the chair. You're not trying to spring him now, are you?"

"Not me."

"Then what's the problem?"

"When he was sentenced there was a dame there to see him off. It may have been his sister. Your paper had a picture of her back, but that's all. If you know any of the photogs who covered the thing, maybe one of them might have clipped a shot of her face.

"Something doing?"

"She might be a witness in something else, but I want to be sure."

"I can check," he said. "Hang on."

Twenty minutes later a clerk came up from the morgue with two four-by-five glossies that showed her face. One was a partial profile, the other a front view. The last one was the best. The coat hinted at the fullness of her body and the wide brim of her hat didn't conceal a face that devoid of makeup was pretty, but with it could have been beautiful. They hadn't printed the picture because Harry Service's face was turned away, but the notation on the back of the photo named her as *Greta Service, sister.* Three others were identified as Harry's lawyer, the D.A. and the owner of the store he was trying to rob.

"Can I have this, Hy?"

"Be my guest," he said without looking up from his notes. "When you going to tell me about it?"

"It's just a little thing. Might be nothing at all."

"Don't con me, kiddo. I've seen you with that look before."

"Maybe I better not play poker."

"Not with me. Or Pat."

I got up and stuck on my hat. "So you want to come along?"

"Not me. I'm cleaning up here and heading for Miami. I know when to cut out. Write me about it when it's over."

"Sure thing," I said. "Thanks."

The Greenwich Village number was a weatherbeaten brownstone that was part of the old scene, a three-story structure that could have been anything once, but had been converted into studio apartments for the artists and writers set. Inside the small foyer I ran my fingertip along the names under the mailboxes, but there was no Greta Service listed. It wasn't surprising. In view of the publicity given her brother, she could have changed her name.

Now it was all legwork and luck. I pushed the first bell button and shoved the door open when the latch began to click. A guy in a pair of paint-stained slacks stuck a tousled head out the door and said, "Yeah?"

"I'm looking for a Greta Service."

He gave me a twisted grin and shook his head. "Now friend, that sure ain't me. I'm the only straight man in this pad. This is a dame you're talking about, ain't it?"

"That's what I was told. She lived here a year and a half ago."

"Before my time, feller. I've only been here six weeks."

"How about one of the other tenants?"

The guy scratched his head and frowned. "Tell you what . . . as far as I know that kookie bunch on the next floor moved in about four months ago. Student type, if you know the kind. Long hair, tight pants and loose, and I mean like loose, man . . . morals. Me, mine are lax, but not loose. They're real screamers up there. Odd jobs and checks from home to keep them away from home. If I was their old man . . ."

"Who else is there?"

He let out a short laugh. "You might try Cleo on the top floor. That is, if she's available for speaking to. She ain't always. They tell me she's been around a while."

"Cleo who?"

"It's *whom*, ain't it?" he said. "Anyway, who cares? I don't think I ever heard any other name."

"Thanks, I'll give it a try."

When he had ducked back behind the door I picked my way up the stairs to the second-floor landing and stood there a few seconds. Inside the apartment a couple was arguing the merits of some obscure musician while another was singing an accompaniment to a scratchy record player. It was only ten A.M., but none of them sounded sober. I took the guy's advice and followed the stairs up to the next floor.

I knocked twice before I heard the languid tap of heels come toward the door. It opened, not the usual few inches restricted by a guard chain women seem to affect, but fully and with a single sweeping motion designed to stun the visitor. It was great theatrical staging.

She stood there, hands against the door jambs, the light from the French windows behind her filtering through the silken kimono, silhouetting the matronly curves under it. Poodle-cut hair framed a face that had an odd, intense beauty that seemed to leap out of dark eyes that were so inquisitive they appeared to reach out and feel you, then decide whether you were good enough to eat or not.

For a second the advantage was hers and all I could do was grin a little bit and say, "Cleo?"

"That's me, stranger." Then the eyes felt me a little more and she added, "You look familiar."

"Mike Hammer"

"Ah, yes." She let a little laugh tinkle from her throat. "The man on the front page." Then she let her hands drop, held one out and took my arm. "Come in. Don't just stand there."

This time I let my own eyes do the feeling. They ran up and down the length of her asking questions of their own.

Cleo laughed again, knowing what I meant. "Don't mind my costuming. I'm doing a self-portrait," she said. "It does kind of rock you at first though, doesn't it?"

"Pretty interesting," I agreed.

She gave a disgusted toss of her head. "Men like you have lived too long. Nothing's new. I could slaughter you." She grinned again and ran her fingers through her hair. "But you should see what it does to the other kind."

"I don't know the other kind."

"Naturally."

She led me inside and slid up on a wooden bar stool in front of an easel while I looked around the room. Unlike most of the village pads, it was a completely professional setup. The windows

40

and skylight were modern and cleverly arranged for maximum efficiency, wall shelves stocked with every necessity, and on the far end, equipment for engraving and etching stretched from one side to the other.

Every wall was covered with framed pictures, some original art, others black and white or full color glossy reproductions. Every one bore the simple signature, *Cleo.*

"Like them?"

I nodded. "Commercial."

"Hell yes," she told me. "The loot is great and I don't go the beatnik route. I don't expect you to recognize them . . . you don't look the type to read women's fashion magazines, but I happen to be one of the best in the field."

I walked over to the easel and stood beside her. The picture she was painting would never make any family magazine. The face and body were hers, all right, but the subject matter was something else. Even unfinished you knew what she was portraying. She was a seductress for hire, promising any man anything he could possibly want, not because money was the object, but because she desired it that way herself. It was a total desire to please and be pleased, but whoever succumbed to the lure was going to be completely devoured with the excesses she could provide to satisfy her own pleasures.

"How about that," I said.

"You got the message?"

"I got the message," I repeated. "Still life."

"Drop dead," she smiled.

"It isn't commercial."

"No? You'd be surprised what some people would buy. But you're right, it isn't commercial . . . or rather, not for sale. I indulge myself in the hobby between assignments. Now, you didn't come up here to talk art."

I walked over and eased myself down into a straight-backed chair. "You ever know Greta Service?"

There was no hesitation. "Sure. She lived downstairs for a while."

"Know her well?"

She shrugged and said, "As well as you ever get to know anybody around here. Except for the old-timers, most are transients or out-of-towners who think the Village is the Left Bank of New York."

"What was she?"

"An out-of-towner. I forget where she came from, but she was doing some modeling work and moved into the Village because it seemed the thing to do and the rent comparatively cheap."

Casually, I asked, "What are you doing here?"

"Me," Cleo smiled, "I like it. I guess I read too many stories about the place years ago too. Right now I'm one of the old-timers which means you've been here over ten years. Only thing is, I'm different."

"Oh?"

"I make money. I can support my habit of fine

foods and a big bar bill. Around here I'm an odd-ball because of it. The others dig my hobby but sneer at my crass commercial works, yet they still take the free drinks and stuff their pockets as well as their stomachs whenever I toss a neighborhood soirée up here." She glanced at me seriously. "What's with this Greta Service?"

"A friend wants to locate her. Got any ideas?"

Cleo thought a moment, then shook her head. "You know about her brother?"

I nodded.

"Not long after that she moved out. As far as I know, she never said a word about where she was going. Her mail piled up in the box downstairs, so apparently she never left a forwarding address."

"How about her friends?"

"Greta wasn't exactly the friendly type. She was . . . well, remote. I saw her with a few men, but it wasn't like . . . well, whether she cared they were there or not. I did get an impression however. Unless they were wealthy, she wasn't interested."

"Gold digger?"

"What an archaic term," Cleo told me. "No, not quite that. She just was determined to get money. Several times she said she had enough of scraping by. It was there to be had if you looked hard enough." Cleo slid off the stool and stretched elegantly, the sheer silk of the kimono pulling taut across the skin beneath it. "She was a determined kid," she said. "She'll make it somehow."

"But how?"

43

"Women have ways if they want something badly enough. There are always hidden talents."

"Yeah, sure," I said.

"Cynic."

"Anybody around here who might know where she'd be?"

She gave me a thoughtful look and said, "Possibly. I'd have to ask around some."

"I'd appreciate it."

Cleo grinned at me. "How much?"

"What're you asking?"

"Maybe you'd like to pose for me."

"Hell, I'm not the still-life type," I said.

"That's what I mean," she said impishly.

I got up with a laugh. "I'm going to squeal to your boss."

"Oh, you'd like her."

"Dames," I said. I walked to the door and turned around. Cleo still had the window at her back and the shadow effect of her body was a tantalizing thing. "I'll check back later," I told her.

"You'd better," she said.

The R. J. Marion Realty Company on Broadway owned the Village building Greta Service had occupied. The receptionist introduced me to a short, balding man named Richard Hardy who handled the downtown rentals and after he waved me to a chair and I explained what I wanted he nodded and said, "Greta Service, yes, I remember her, but I'm afraid I can't help you at all.

"No forwarding address?"

"Nothing at all. We held her mail here for a month before returning it to the senders, hoping she might notify us, but there was no word whatsoever. Incidentally, this isn't exactly uncommon. Some of the tenants down there are, well, peculiar. They come and go and sometimes don't want anyone to know where they've been."

"Any of that mail here now?"

"No . . . but it wouldn't help anyway. It was mostly bills from some of the better stores, a few from model agencies and a lot of circulars. Her rent and utilities were paid up, so we didn't think much of it."

I thanked the guy, left him to a desk full of paperwork and went down to the street. New York still had her gray hat on and the air had a chilly smell to it. I edged to the curb side and followed the crowd up to my corner and headed toward the office.

Velda was on the phone when I walked in. She finished talking and hung up. "How'd you make out?"

I gave her what information I had and picked up a couple of folders from her desk. "What's this?"

"Background on Helen Poston and Maxine Delaney. I thought you'd want it. They're mostly newspaper clips, but they cover as much as the police have. I reached some people in the Poston girl's home town who knew her . . . the school superintendent, the principal, two teachers and the

45

man who sold her a used car. She had a good reputation as far as her work was concerned, but I got the impression that teaching wasn't her main ambition in life.

I glanced up from the folder and stared at her. "Like how?"

"Nothing definite . . . it was an impression. The car salesman was the one who put his finger on it. You know the type . . . a real swinger ready to sound off about anybody. He was the one who said he'd like to see her in a bikini. She bought the car to make a trip and seemed pretty excited about getting away from the home town and all he could think of was a small-town teacher in a big city having a ball away from the prying eyes of the school board. I said I was doing a feature story on her and he made sure I spelled his name right."

"And Maxine Delaney?"

"I called Vernie in L.A. and he checked with the arresting officer who picked her up. His opinion was that she was one of the lost tribe who inhabit the movie colony with stars in their eyes until disillusionment sets in, then she didn't give a damn any more. Bob Sabre reached the Chicago outfit she posed for and said they didn't bother with her because she didn't project. Nice face and body, but she lacked that intangible something. She still thought she was a star and played it that way."

"Two of a kind," I said.

"There's a similarity." She pinched her lower

lip between her teeth a moment, then said, "Mike . . ."

"What?"

"I can see the green on the redhead, but that black didn't fit the blonde Poston girl. She wasn't the type."

"They change when they hit the big town, kid."

"Everybody said she was extremely conservative."

"That was at home. There weren't any eyes watching her here."

"Could there be a connection?"

"If there is, it'll come out. Right now I want you to check all the charge accounts at the better stores and see what you can get on Greta Service. She might have left a forwarding address with their billing departments. I can't see a dame giving up charge accounts or lousing up her credit if it can be avoided."

Velda grinned up at me. "You going to leave a forwarding address?"

"Yeah," I said, "yours. I'll call in later."

"Thanks a lot."

"Only because I love you, baby."

"Oh boy," she said quietly and reached for the phone.

Donald Harney had an office on the ninth floor of the Stenheim Building, sharing space with three other lawyers who hadn't made the high-income cases yet. The legal library was all secondhand and it was plain that any attempt at putting up a front was a lost cause a long time ago. The community receptionist told me to go right on in and I pushed through the door to his private cubicle.

Harney didn't stand on ceremony in his own back yard. He sat there in his shirtsleeves with a pencil over his ear editing a brief, shoved his hair out of his eyes and got up for a handshake. Our last meeting at Harry Service's trial had been short, on the witness stand, and then only for a few perfunctory questions regarding his arrest. It had been a plea of guilty and his concern was getting Harry off with as light a sentence as possible.

When he sat back relaxed he said, "What brings you here, Mike? My client bust out?"

"Harry isn't the type," I told him. "He'd rather sweat out a parole. Look . . . I'd like some facts about him."

"It's still privileged information."

"I know, but it concerns the welfare of your client . . . and mine." I grinned at him. "Funny as it sounds, Harry asked me to do him a favor." I held out the note he had sent and let Harney read it over, then tucked it back in my wallet.

"How'd he get that to you?"

"Guys in stir can think up a lot of ways. Know anything about his sister?"

Harney squinted and swung in his chair. "Harry's case was assigned to me by the court. He didn't have any funds to provide for a defense. The trial lasted three days only because the prosecution was trying to tie Harry into a few other unsolved robberies. The last day his sister appeared out of nowhere, damn well upset, too. Apparently they had been pretty close in their earlier days, then split up after their parents died and hadn't kept in touch."

"It was too late to do anything then."

Harney shrugged and nodded. "She seemed to blame herself . . . a sort of maternal instinct coming out. When they were kids he was quite a hero to her. Later he helped her out financially when she was off working."

"What did she do?"

"She never said. Anyway, the day Harry was sentenced she told him she was going to make sure they never had to worry again, that she'd get things ready for his release . . . you know, the usual emotional outburst."

"Was it?"

Harney gave me a puzzled look. "Well, she seemed serious enough, but I've been through those situations before. It sounds good at the time, but how the hell can a dame alone do all that?"

"There are ways."

"Which brings us up to why you're here."

"Yeah. She's missing and Harry's worried. Tell me, have you seen him in prison?"

"Twice. I went up there on other business and took the time to say hello."

"He mention anything?" I asked him.

"Only that things were fine, his sister came to see him often and he was working toward a parole. You can't always tell, but he seemed convinced that crime was more trouble than it was worth. In fact, he even asked about you. Once he called you a 'nice bastard' because you could have killed him and didn't."

I stuck a butt in my mouth and lit it. "There's an odd factor here, you know?"

"The way Harry Service contacted you?"

"He could have gone through you."

Harney let out a grunt and shook his head. "You know those guys, Mike. I represent the law. Face it, in your own peculiar way, you don't. With your reputation you're closer to being one of their own kind. I can see his point. Now, what can I do to help out?"

"Get a line on Greta Service and buzz me." I grinned a little and added, "I'll split the fee when Harry gets out."

For a few seconds Harney studied my face. "You got more going than Harry Service, haven't you?"

"I don't know. There's a possibility. At least we can wrap up this bit for Old Harry."

"You don't owe him anything."

"He asked me for a favor."

A small twitch of humor touched the corner of his mouth. "You tough guys are all alike."

"Will do?" I asked.

"Will do," he said.

Greenwich Village is a state of mind. Like Hollywood. There really isn't such a place left any more. It exists in the memories of the old ones and in the misconceptions of the new ones. It's on the map and in the vocabulary, but the thing that made Hollywood and the Village has long since gone and thousands prowl the area where they once were, looking for the reality but finding only the shadow.

A few landmarks are still around; the streets do their jig steps and the oddball characters wrapping up their life on canvas or in unpublished manuscripts are attractions for the tourists. But the city is too big and too fast-growing to contain a sore throat and coughed-up phlegm. The world of commerce has moved in, split it with the beatniks who clutched for a final handhold, and tolerates it because New York still needs a state of mind to retain its image while the computers finally take over.

For those who lived there, night, like Gaul, was divided into three parts. The realists occupied it early, the spectators came to browse during the second shift, then the others waited for the all-clear to sound and came out of the dream world to indulge their own fantasies.

I sat in a smoke-shrouded bar nursing a highball, watching the third stage drift in. Since midnight I had been buying the bartender a drink every third round and the last hour he had been getting friendly enough to pour me a legitimate jolt and spend time down at my end growling about the type of trade he had to put up with. After a couple paid for beer in nickels and pennies he came back, mopped down in front of me, moving my bills out of the way and said, "What are you doing here? You're from uptown, ain't you?"

"Way uptown."

"This place gives me the creeps," he said. "I shoulda stayed with the Department of Sanitation. My old lady didn't like being married to a garbage man. Now look. I serve garbage to garbage. Damn, what a life."

"It's tough all over."

"You looking for action?"

"That I can get uptown."

His eyes ran over my face. "I seen you before. You with the Vice Squad?"

"Hell no."

"Too bad. You'd have a ball in this place only you'd never have jail room." He stopped and squinted at me. "Where did I see you?"

I flipped one of my cards out of my coat pocket and held it out.

"Ain't that something," he said. "I knew I seen you someplace. What's with this joint?"

"The end of the road, looks like. I've been trying to run down Greta Service all night."

"So why didn't you ask?"

"You know her?"

The guy hunched his shoulders and spread his hands out. "She used to come by here some. Lived a few blocks over, I think. She in a jam?"

"Not that I know of. Her brother wants to locate her."

"The one who got pinched? Hey . . . you were

on that job, weren't you?"

"I nailed him. Now he wants me to find her."

"Boy, she ain't been around a while. She moved outa her pad down here, but came back sometimes for hellos. Went native once."

"What?"

"You know, hanging on the arm of some gook with a funny hat. He wasn't no American. The guy had bucks and shelled it out, but when she started mixing it with some of her old friends he made her cut out."

"Recognize him?"

The guy picked up the bar rag and mopped at nothing in particular. "Hell, who knows from who around here? They all look alike. Most of that type are down at the Flagstaff anyway. I don't pay no attention to nobody nohow. Stay out of trouble like that."

"Ever see her with anybody else?"

"Couple of times she was with the dykes what come in, only in this joint that ain't unusual. She'd sit with some of the local kids for a few drinks sometimes. Can't say I ever seen her with anyone special except that gook." He picked up my glass, built me a fresh drink on the house and set it down in front of me. He let me taste it, nodded approvingly, and said, "Come to think of it, I stopped by Lew Michi's place after I closed up here and she was with some good-looking dame and one of those foreigners then too. This one didn't wear a gook hat, but he was real native."

"How's that?"

He made another gesture with his hands and said, "You know, dark like, maybe one of those Hindoos or something. They was having a pretty good time, laughing and talking. That was some broad she was with, a real doll. Plenty expensive, too. Some of them tourists come down here dressed like a party at the Ritz."

"Remember when that was?"

The bartender frowned, reached back in thought and told me, "Long time ago. I don't remember seeing her after that at all. Guess she moved out."

I finished the drink and slid a couple of singles across the bar to him. "Not much I can do here then. Thanks for the talk."

"No trouble. Come back any time. Some nights this place gets real jumpy."

I grinned at him. "I bet."

Outside, the night people were rendezvousing on the corners, ready to swing into the usual routine. Headquarters was a bar or a restaurant where they could sip coffee or a beer and talk interminably about nothing anyone else could understand.

A couple of squad cars cruised by slowly, the cops scanning faces, checking each place for trouble before going on. Nobody paid any attention to them at all. I reached Seventh Avenue, turned right and walked south a block toward a cab stand ready to call it a night.

Then I saw Cleo sitting at the end of the bar on the corner and pushed in through the door and sat down beside her.

"Hello, big man," she said without looking up from her paper

"Got eyes in the back of your head?"

"Nope. Just good peripheral vision." Then she folded the paper with a throaty chuckle and flipped it aside. "You're still haunting our house."

"It's not like the old days, Cleo."

"Things change. Find out anything about Greta?"

"Not much. She didn't leave much to start from." I waved the bartender over and told him to bring me a Four Roses and ginger ale. "You ever know who she worked for?"

Cleo gave me a small negative shake of her head. "She was registered with most of the agencies. I know she got jobs here and there . . . at least enough to support herself. Most of them were with the garment industry, modeling for the trades. You really have to hustle to make a buck in that business. I sent her up to see Dulcie once. . . ."

"Who?" I interrupted.

"Dulcie McInnes, my boss. Super fashion editor of the Proctor Group. Money, society, international prominence among the fashion set who buy three-thousand-dollar gowns. Greta got her interview, but it ended there. Her appearance was earthy rather than ethereal and the Proctor girls have to be gaunt, long-necked and flat-chested. Greta photographed like a pin-up doll."

55

"Tell me something," I said. "How much do these kids make?"

"If you're one of the top twenty you can climb into the fifty-thousand-a-year bracket. Otherwise you stay in the crowd, squeeze out a hundred or two a week for the few years nature lets your face stay unwrinkled and hope for a break or somebody who wants to marry you."

"How about you, kid?"

Cleo gave me another of those deep chuckles and said, "I made my own breaks and when it comes to men, well, after two sour early marriages, I'll take them when I want them."

"You'll fall."

"It'll take a guy like you to do it." She reached over and pinched the back of my hand. "I'm the aggressive type, watch out."

I tasted the drink and put it down. "Think Greta could have lit out with some guy?"

She made a wry face and shook her head. "Greta had more on her mind than men, I told you. She was the money type and had enough to attract it." She paused and picked up her drink. "How far are you going to go to locate her?"

"Beats me, kid. She had a pretty big head start."

"Look, there's one thing about the city . . . pretty soon you bump into someone you know. Maybe some of the gang around here might have seen her. If it means that much to you we can tour a few of the places she played in."

"I've had enough gin mills for one night."

Cleo finished her drink and slid off the stool with a rustle of nylon, a funny little smile playing around her mouth. "Uh-uh, big man. Little Greta had peculiar tastes. The oddball intellectuals were more to her liking."

"Lead on," I said.

If there was a host, nobody pointed him out. Introductions were a casual affair of no last names and preoccupied acceptance. The smell of weed mixed in the tobacco smoke that hung in the air like a gray smog and a few were already flying away into a dream world on something stronger.

Cleo and I drifted around the fringes a few minutes before she leaned over and whispered, "The weekly gathering of the clan, big man. Greta made the meetings pretty often. Some of them would have known her. Go ahead and cruise. Maybe you'll come up with something. Give me a nod when you've had enough."

Most of the two dozen crammed into the apartment sprawled on the floor listening to the pair strumming guitars on the window seat. A cropped-haired girl in tight jeans sang a bitter song against the world with her eyes squeezed tight, her hands clenched in balled fists of protest.

I gave up after the second time around and joined the two guys at the makeshift bar back in the kitchen and made myself a decent drink for a change. An empty fishbowl beside the bottles was partly filled with assorted change and few lone singles, waiting for contributions to help pay the freight. I dug out a five, dropped it in and the guy with the beard grinned and said, "Well, well, a banker in our midst." He lifted his glass in a toast. "We salute thee. That denomination doesn't appear very often around here."

I winked at him and tried the highball. "Nice party," I said.

"Hell, it stinks. It was better when we had that horsy belly dancer up for laughs." He tugged at his beard and grimaced. "You dig this gravy?"

"Nope."

"You didn't look like the type."

"I can give you the first ten lines of 'Gunga Din,'" I said.

He let out a short laugh and took a long pull from his beer bottle. "I must be getting old. Guys like you are easier to read. Me, I'm scratching thirty-four and still going to college, only now the freshman cap doesn't fit too well and I'm beginning to think that maybe my old man was right after all. I should have gone into the business with him. When you get that attitude, the kick is gone." He paused reflectively. "Maybe I'll start off with a shave."

"Try a haircut too."

"The freshman cap wouldn't fit," he laughed. "How'd you make it here?"

"Cleo brought me."

"Ah, yes. The lady of the loins. Some great stories are told about that one, but methinks it's all talk. Not a Simon around who wouldn't want to sample her pies. You tried it for size yet?"

"Nope."

"Ha. That's a different answer. Anyone else would have happily lied about it. Intend to?"

"I haven't thought about it."

"Brother rat, with an attitude like that, you can't miss. Cleo just can't stand indifference. How'd you ever meet her?"

"Looking for Greta Service. She lived in the same building."

The guy gave me a surprised glance. "Greta? Good grief. She's long gone." His eyes ran up and down me. "She give you the brush too?"

"Never even met her."

"That's good. Guys flipped for that one and she wouldn't go the route. A few hearts are still bleeding around here. Sol saw her once uptown but she shook him loose in a hurry. Didn't want anything to do with her old buddies."

"Who's he?"

He indicated a lanky kid in a red plaid shirt curled up against the wall, chin propped in his hands while he contemplated the trio whanging out the folk songs. "Wait a minute, I'll go get him."

Sol Renner turned out to be a sometimes-writer of ads and captions for the women's trades and had met Greta Service through a mutual account. My story was that I had a message from a friend who had a job lined up for her, but Sol grimaced and told me to forget it.

"She didn't need a job when I saw her last. She was coming out of a fancy restaurant with some joe, all decked out in furs and diamonds and all I got was a quick 'hello, glad to see you' and out. I asked her if she heard about Helen Poston, but she just gave me a funny look and nodded, then got into a cab."

"Helen Poston?"

"Yeah. Crazy kook drowned herself. She and Greta did a couple of jobs for Signoret Fashions where I worked and kind of hit it off like dames do. Guess they were friendlier than I thought. So I boo-booed. She sure picked herself a beauty, though."

"Who?"

"Greta," he said. "The duck she was with was a Charlie Chan type, short, dark and dumpy with b.b. eyes and a mustache. He hustled her in the cab in a hell of a hurry."

"Got any idea where I could find her?"

He grinned and said, "Try New York."

"Great."

"Maybe some of the others might know?"

"Ixnay. I'm the only one around here who saw her. The kid's found her mark. My guess is she doesn't want to be disturbed. Anyway, she's not with the working masses any more, that's for sure."

The singers got started on a new theme about war and I finished my drink. Cleo was cornered in the alcove by two straggly-haired kids sucking on beer bottles, trying their damndest to make man talk. I eased them apart; smiling so as not to hurt their feelings and took Cleo's arm.

"Time to go, sugar."

One of the kids grabbed my hand and said, "Hey!" indignantly, so I wrapped my fingers around his forearm and squeezed a little bit. "Yes?"

My smile showed all the teeth and he read me right. "Nothing," he said, so I let him go. Cleo forced back a laugh and hooked her arm under mine and we headed for the door.

"Big man," she said. "Big, big man. Come home for coffee. I have something to show you."

I kicked the door shut and she flowed into my arms, her mouth a wild little volcano trying to pull me into its core. Deliberately, she took my hand, pressed it against the warmth of her belly, then forced it up to cup her breast. Beneath my fingers she hardened, her body twitching spasmodically, pressing against me in a plain language of desire.

Very gently I pushed her away and held her hands in mine. Her eyes were full of soft fire, lovely and wise, her lips moist and trembling. She looked at me for a long second, then said, "No coffee?"

"Rain check?"

She smiled ruefully and touched my face with her fingertips. "How can you do this to me, big man?"

"It isn't easy."

"The next time I'll make it real hard for you."

"Shut up," I grinned.

61

chapter four

I came in out of the rain, threw my coat over the back of the desk chair and picked up the coffee Velda had waiting for me. She let me finish half of it before she came over and laid a two-page report down in front of me. "Rough night?"

Women. I didn't bother playing her game. "Not bad. I got a line on Greta Service."

"So did I."

"Brief me," I said.

"She had six hundred dollars in charges she had been paying off monthly. She cleaned them all up at once with cash payments, didn't draw on any more purchases and never left a forwarding address. One woman in the credit department knew her from when she was a saleswoman and waited on her. From what she hinted at, Greta Service was wearing finer clothes than the store supplied. Where were *you* last night?"

"Working." I synopsized the details of last night for her, emphasizing the relationship Greta Service had had with Helen Poston. Velda made a few notes on a scratch pad, her face serious. "Want me to follow it up?"

"Yeah, ask around her neighborhood. They'd

remember a suicide all right. Lay on a few bucks if you have to grease anybody. As far as they're concerned, you're a reporter doing a follow-up yarn. Just be careful."

"Like you?" She gave me a poke with her elbow.

I looked up at her and a teasing smile was playing with the corner of her mouth. "Okay, I won't bug you," she said. "Only you could have put on a clean shirt without lipstick on the collar."

"I'm a show off," I said.

"That you are, chum. Sometimes I could kill you." She refilled my cracked cup from the quart container and asked, "What do you think?"

"A pattern's showing. Greta came up with money from some area. It looks more like she found a sponsor than a job."

"That's what the credit manager suggested. Did you check the m.p.'s with Pat?"

"No good. Who'd report her missing? Harry came directly to me. From now on it's legwork around probable places she might spend time in."

"Would they recognize her from that photo Hy gave you? It isn't very good."

"No, but I know where I can get a better one," I told her.

Velda picked up her coffee and sat on the arm of the chair beside me. "And I'll do the work while you carouse . . . is that it?"

"That's what I got you for, baby," I said cheerfully.

"You're asking for it," she growled back. "All this for a con."

"It goes further than that. Has Pat called?"

"No, but Hy has. He washed out the Miami trip for a few days to do a couple of features on Mitch Temple. You'd better buzz him."

"Okay." I finished the coffee and reached for my coat. "I'll check in this afternoon."

"Mike . . ."

"What, kitten?"

"It's those negligees. . . ."

"Don't worry, I didn't forget. Mitch Temple wasn't killed for nothing. Pat'll run that lead right into the ground. When he has something I'll know about it."

The Proctor Group was located in the top half of a new forty-story building it had just built on Sixth Avenue, a glass and concrete monument to commercialism with the sterile atmosphere of a hospital.

Dulcie McInnes was listed on the lobby directory as Executive Fashion Editor with offices on the top floor. I got in the elevator along with a half dozen women who eyed me speculatively and seemed to pass knowing little glances between them when I pushed the top button.

It was a woman's world, all right. The decor was subtle pastels, the windows draped with feminine elegance and footsteps were muted by the thick pale green carpeting. Expensive oil paintings decorated the walls of the reception room, but something seemed to be missing.

✓ The two harried little men I saw scuttled around like mice in a house full of cats, forcing badgered smiles at the dominant females who wore their hats like crowns, performing their insignificant tasks meticulously, gratefully acknowledging the curt nods of their overlords with abundant thank you's. What was missing were the whips on the wall. The damn place was a harem and they were the eunuchs. One looked at me as if I were a peddler who came to the front door of the mansion, was about to ask me my business when he caught the reproving eye of the receptionist and drifted off without a word.

She was a gray woman with the hard eyes and stern mouth of the dean of a girls' school. Her expression was one of immediate rejection and no compromise. She was the guardian dog at the portals of the castle, not there to greet, but to discourage any entry. Her suit had an almost military cut to it and her voice held a tone of total hostility.

"May I help you?"

Help? She was wanting to know what the hell I was doing there in the first place.

"I'd like to see Dulcie McInnes," I said.

"Do you have an appointment?"

"Nope."

"Then I'm afraid it's impossible." The dismissal was as fast as that. To make it more pointed, she went back to sorting her mail.

Only she had the wrong mouse this time. I

walked to the side of the desk, leaned over and whispered in her ear. Her eyes went wide open almost to the point of bursting, her face a dead white, then a slow flush began at her neck and suffused her cheeks and the stammer that came out of her mouth had a little squeak to it.

"Now," I said.

Her head bobbed and she tried to wet her lips with a tongue just as dry. She pushed back from the desk, got up and edged around me nervously and stepped inside the door marked *Private* beside her. In ten seconds she was back, holding the door open timorously to let me in, then closed it quickly with a short gasp of horror, when I grinned at her.

The woman on the couch wasn't what I expected at all. She had a mature beauty only middle age can bring when nature cooperates with fashion demands and scientific treatment. A touch of gray added a silvery quality to hair that fell in soft waves around a face that held a gentle tan. Her mouth was full and rich, curved in a welcoming smile. She put the layout sheets on the coffee table and stood up, sensing my immediate approval of the way the black sheath dress encompassed the swell of her breasts and dipped into the hollow and flare of her hips.

But it was her eyes that got you. They were a bright, unnatural emerald green full of laughter.

"Miss McInnes?"

Her teeth sparkled white under her smile and she held her hand out. "Whatever did you say to

Miss Tabor? She was absolutely terrified."

"Maybe I'd better not repeat it."

"She never even got your name."

Her hand was firm and warm in mine, enthusiastic for the few moments she held it. "Mike Hammer," I said. "I'm a private investigator."

"Now that's a novelty up here," she laughed. "No wonder Miss Tabor was so upset. Haven't I read about you?"

"Probably."

She walked back to the couch and sat down, held out a box of cigarettes to me when I took the chair opposite her and lit us both with an ornate gold lighter.

"You've got me curious about your visit. Who's being investigated?"

I blew out a cloud of smoke and took the photograph from my pocket. "Nothing spectacular. I'm trying to find this woman. Greta Service . . . she's a model."

Dulcie McInnes took the photograph from my hand and studied it a minute. "Should I know her?"

"Probably not. She applied here for photographic work one time at Cleo's suggestion and . . ."

"Cleo?" Her head tilted with a gesture of interest. "She's one of our finest contributors."

"Think you may have some test pictures of her?"

"Undoubtedly. Just a moment." She picked up the phone, pressed a button on the base and said,

"Marsha? See if we have any photos of Greta Service in our personnel files. No, she's a model. Bring them up, please."

When she hung up she asked, "Did she work for us?"

"Opinion is that Greta was, well . . . a little too stacked for high fashion jobs."

"Luckily for us we're only concerned with the woman's opinion. You men . . . all you want is pin-ups."

I looked at her and felt my mouth twist into a smile.

She threw back her head and laughed, her eyes sparkling in the light. "No, I'm not the high fashion type either, thank goodness. I'd hate to have to starve myself into a size six."

"I don't think that would help much either. When you're endowed, you're endowed. Don't knock it."

"Words like that rarely pass through these portals." Her eyes were filled with a mocking challenge. "I assume you're an expert on these matters."

"I haven't heard any complaints."

Before she could answer there was a knock on the door and a tall, slim girl walked in with a folder, handed it to her boss and threw a nervous little glance toward me before she left. "You made quite an impression outside," Dulcie McInnes said and handed me the folder after examining it.

Inside was a typed résumé listing Greta Service's statistics and qualifications. Her address was the one in the Village. Several news clippings from the garment industry's trade papers showed her in various costumes with her face partially obscured by either a coat collar or wide-brimmed hat, and there were four composite photos with the Proctor Group stamp on the back.

Greta Service was all that was said about her. No dress could do justice to a body that was so obviously made for a bikini. There was no way of erasing the odd, sensual appeal of her face so beautifully framed by long jet black hair, and no matter how she posed, you got the impression she would rather be naked than in a dress of any price.

"You see it too?" she asked me.

"Lovely."

"I didn't mean that. She just isn't a Proctor Girl. It's one of the hazards of the business."

I picked the best of the lot and held it up. "Can I have this?"

"Certainly, if it will help. We keep the negatives on file downstairs. Occasionally we do have requests from certain manufacturers for this type, but not often."

I rolled it up and slipped it in my pocket. "Think anybody here might know anything about her?"

"I doubt it," she said. "Her application date was quite a few months ago and they interview girls daily down there. Women are such a common commodity in this business you can't tell one from the other after a while. I remember getting Cleo's note about this girl, but I passed it on to personnel to handle. She wasn't the first Cleo submitted and we have used several others she suggested. Top-notch free-lancers like Cleo aren't easy to find and they usually make a good choice. In this case, I imagine Cleo was doing a little wishful thinking. The Service girl would do better with one of the men's magazines."

"What's the going rate with them?"

She shrugged, thought a moment and said, "Only a fraction of ours. Once a Proctor Girl, the sky's the limit. Quite a few have wound up in Hollywood."

I got up and pulled my coat on. "That's it then. Thanks for your time, Miss McInnes."

"Glad you came." Her emerald eyes seemed to dance with my own. "It's made for an enjoyable morning." A tiny furrow creased her forehead. "Would you mind letting me know if you find her?"

"Sure."

"It's ridiculous, I know, but I get a maternal feeling about these girls. It isn't a bit easy for them at all."

She held out her hand and I wrapped my own around it. I squeezed too hard, but she didn't wince and her own grip was firm and pleasing. "You'll hear from me," I said.

"Don't forget."

The receptionist made a frightened, crablike

move to get out of the way when I stepped through the door, her face flushing again when I looked at her. Then she sniffed with indignation and faked ignoring me. She was the only one. The other few in the room looked at me with open curiosity, their eyes full of speculation.

I pushed the down button and waited, listening to the rush of air in the elevator well behind the door. The noise stopped and the doors parted sullenly. A swarthy man clutching a black attaché case stepped out, his sleepy eyes sweeping over me carelessly before he headed toward the reception desk. I got in and pressed the lobby button, picked up several employees and a few who were obviously models on the way down and reached the street smelling of assorted imported perfumes.

Sixth Avenue had lost its identity over the last ten years. It was an empire now.

The lunch crowd had left the Blue Ribbon Restaurant when I met Hy Gardner and we had the corner table in the bar to ourselves. I sat with my back to the wall while Hy dug out a sheaf of notes and laid them on the table while he fished for words. He looked like a guy who couldn't scratch his itch and finally he said, "What the hell are you into now, Mike?"

"Ease off, buddy," I told him. "Clue me in first."

"Okay." He sat back and shoved his glasses up on his forehead. "You're on top of the Delaney kill, you had a contact with Mitch Temple before

71

he was knocked off, then you were there with Pat at the apartment after Mitch was bumped and we couldn't even get in."

"Wait a minute . . ."

"Quit dicing. One of the guys saw you take the side exit out. But you wanted something on Greta Service and if you think I don't think this is all part of one of your packages, you're crazy."

"Hy . . ."

"Look," he interrupted, "my Miami trip is loused up, one of our own guys got killed and you're playing footsies with me. Since when?"

"Can you cool it if I spell it out?"

"What am I, a kid? Man, after all we've been through . . ."

"All right, I'm not even sure there's a connection." I took five minutes and laid out the details for him while he jotted them down on the back of one of his papers. When I got done I said, "Make anything of it?"

"According to Harry Service his sister knew both the Poston and the Delaney girl. Your report verified the Poston tie-in, anyway. In their business it wouldn't be unusual — they probably have plenty of mutual friends. Dozens of them line up for one job and they're always meeting at the agencies. So far as you know, Greta Service is around someplace and the only one worried is her brother, and that's because he heard about the two deaths and the fact that his sister knew both of them."

"Greta disappeared," I said.

"Not disappeared," Hy stated. "Her immediate whereabouts are unknown. You think that's something new in this town? Hell, let a broad in that racket hook a guy who'll keep her in minks and she'll drop the old gang in a second. Since when do I tell you that?"

"You're not, friend. I got the same picture. It's just that I got a funny feeling about it."

"Oh boy," Hy said. "Oh, boy. I don't even like you when you get that look. You'll screw the works up for sure."

"Maybe. What's the news on Temple?"

Hy pulled his glasses down on the end of his nose and peered at me over them. "You don't hit one of us that easily. It gets everybody edgy and we have too many inside sources we can work. In our own way we're like cops. News is where the trouble is and we're right there. Right now everybody is in the field on this assignment and little things are drifting in the cops never even heard about."

"Like what?"

"Mitch was around too long not to keep a daily record. Bobby Dale dug it up in his personal effects in the office. The only thing hot he had going was the Poston and Delaney tie-in. He left a page full of speculation about that, including Pat Chambers' request through you to lay off running it."

"Don't blame Pat for that."

"I'm not. But it didn't stop Mitch from pushing the angle. He hit every damn store he could find who sold negligees like the ones those

73

kids wore and spent over three hundred bucks making purchases in various ones. The boxes started arriving at the office the day he was killed."

"What came of it?"

"He found something that killed him, that's what. The day he was knifed he was all excited about something and spent a full hour in the morgue file going through stock photographs. He didn't pull any or there would have been a record of it and the attendant there didn't notice what section he was working in so we can't point it up from there."

"Any record of that?"

"It either happened too fast or he was too excited to put it down."

"That doesn't fit him at all."

"I know. Dale said he kept a private reference on him at all times."

"Nothing like that was found on the body."

"That doesn't mean it wasn't there. The position he died in was reaching for his coat. All he grabbed was that handkerchief, but he could have been trying to protect those papers. Whoever killed him simply lifted the stuff."

"But they couldn't be sure he didn't make a duplicate copy," I reminded him.

"It was a chance they took and it paid off. Right now everybody's backtracking Mitch's movements and something will show sooner or later. One thing we just found out was that Mitch made four calls to Norman Harrison, the political columnist on his paper. Norm wasn't home and his answering service took the message to call back. Mitch died before he could reach him. Ordinarily, Mitch and Norm rarely saw each other, so the request was kind of odd."

I went to say something, but Hy held up his hand. "Wait, that isn't all. The day he was poking around in the morgue file Mitch sent a note by messenger to a man named Ronald Miller. He's an engineer for Pericon Chemicals in their foreign division. We contacted him in Cairo and he said Mitch wanted to see him on an important matter, but he was leaving for Egypt that day and couldn't make it. He didn't have any idea of what Mitch wanted, either. Their relationship was normal . . . they had served in the army together, got together occasionally and Mitch reviewed a couple of books this Miller wrote on his experiences in the Far East."

"It makes sense?"

"I pulled the books from the library and went through them. One was an adventure novel and the other a technical travelogue. Neither sold very well. There wasn't a single thing in either one that fits this case."

"How long ago did he write them?"

"About ten years back."

"Nothing new since then?"

"No. Why?"

"Maybe he was intending to write another one."

"So what?"

75

"He could be an authority on something by now," I said.

"What's on your mind?"

"I don't know yet. How much of this has Pat got?"

"Everything. We're cooperating right down the line."

I grinned at him. "Late enough to get a head start, but cooperating."

"We're in business too," Hy agreed. "We still know the law on withholding evidence."

"And you decide what's evidence?"

For the first time Hy let a smile break through. "You ought to know, Mike. Now, where do you go from here?"

"Looking for Greta Service."

"Still on that kick."

"It's the only one I got."

"Suppose it leads to Mitch?"

"He was my friend too, Hy."

"Yeah. Maybe you're right. It's better if we cover all the angles. There's no reason for anybody else to take it from that end except you. I hope you come up with something."

I took the photo of Greta Service from my pocket and held it out to Hy. "Your bunch can help out. How about running off a batch of these and passing them around. Somebody might spot her around Manhattan. And get the original back to my office. I'd like an excuse to see that McInnes doll again when I hand it back."

Hy nodded and grinned. "Not that it'll do you

any good, kid. She's class and you don't fit in that kind of company. You'd have to wear a monkey suit and there wouldn't be any place to hide that damn gun you carry."

Pat met me in his office, his hair mussed and shadows under his eyes, looking like he had been up all night. He said, "Sit down," answered the phone twice, then leaned back in his chair and wiped the back of his hand across his face. "Sometimes I wonder if it's worth it."

"Who's on your back now?"

"You must be kidding. I told you this was an election year. Everybody's passing the buck this time. That Temple kill really stirred the fudge."

"Got anything on it yet?"

He shook his head slowly. "Nothing but boxes of women's nightgowns. We hit all the stores they were bought at and most of the salesgirls remembered selling them, but that's about all. Mitch told the girls he was trying to match one a friend bought for his wife and looked for a description of anyone who bought either black or green, but both colors were so popular the girls couldn't come up with anything concrete."

"Why did he bother buying them then?"

"Got me. Probably just to make it look good. Come here, take a look."

The office next to Pat's was empty, but the desk and chair were piled high with empty boxes and a table along the wall was covered with a mound of filmy garments. I went over and separated them, looking at the labels. None were expensive, but the designs were clearly erotic and not intended for the average housewife. Half the pile were black numbers, the rest all shades of red, green and blue with two canary yellow styles.

"Find out which one he bought last?"

"No. Four of the sales slips were dated the same day he died and all were bought in the morning, but nobody could pinpoint the time. Each one of those stores sold a bunch of these things to men and women the same day. We have a team out trying to nail something down, but all we get is a big, fat zero. Why the hell do these things have to be so complicated?"

"Wish I could help."

"Don't do me any favors," Pat said. "I'm still getting nudged by the brains upstairs about how you happened to be the one to find the Delaney girl."

"What's new on her?"

"One thing for sure . . . neither she nor the Poston girl were identified as buyers of those gowns. We got a make on the Delaney kid by way of left field. About a month ago Vice raided a pornographic photography ring selling sixteen-millimeter stag reels and she was one of the featured players. One of our guys recognized her. The ones who sold the stuff couldn't put a finger on the ones who filmed it, but there was a scene with a window in the background that spotted certain buildings and we were able to locate the hotel they made it in. Right now we have a partial description of the ones who occupied the place and have the hotel covered in case they show again."

"Fat chance. That bunch shift around."

"It's the only chance we have. Dames who make money that way don't pay social security and rarely use their own names. We still got the body on ice. She has one distant relative in Oregon who wants nothing to do with the situation, so there we stand."

"And the Poston woman?"

"You know that angle."

"Don't tell me you aren't digging into probable sources of the poison that might have killed her."

Pat relaxed and grinned at me. "You think too much, Mike," he said. "Sure, we're on it, the Washington agencies have been notified, but the possibilities of getting a lead are so remote I'm not hoping we'll get the answer that way. The M.E. got off some letters to friends in the profession who share the same hobby. He thinks they might be able to supply the answers if anybody has imported that particular drug."

"This deal has some peculiar sexual connotations," I said.

"Most of them have."

"But not like this."

"So far nobody knows they're tied in yet. We're not even sure ourselves. Luckily, the papers are cooperating."

"What happens if they break it first?"

"All hell breaks loose. Think you can use a partner?"

"Any time," I laughed.

"Which brings us to why you came up here in the first place."

I said, "Remember Harry Service?"

Pat nodded.

"He wants me to find his sister. She hasn't contacted him in a long time."

"*You?* He wants *you* to do this?"

"Come on, Pat, he isn't the kind to go to the cops."

"How'd he reach you?"

"Supposing I forget you asked that question."

Pat gave me a disgusted look and said, "Okay, okay. What do you want from me?"

"A letter from the brass getting me in to see Harry. Somebody in the front office has got to be the friendly type."

"Not as far as you're concerned."

"I can push it if I have to."

"I know you can. Just don't. Let me see what I can do." He gave me a quizzical glance and stuck his hands deep into his pockets. "One thing, old buddy. And tell me true. Harry contacted *you,* right?"

"If you don't believe it I can show you how."

"Never mind."

"Why?" I asked him.

"Because if you initiated the contact I'd say it was tying into my immediate business."

My laugh didn't sound too convincing, but Pat bought it. "You know me," I said.

"That's what I'm afraid of."

The attendant at the morgue file of the paper was a crackly little old guy who used to be one of the best rewrite men on the staff until the demands of age caught up with him. Now he was content to spend his time among the artifacts of journalism, complaining about the new generation and how easy they had it.

I said, "Hi, Biff," and he squinted my way, fished for his glasses and got them on his nose.

"Mike Hammer, I'll be damned." He held out a gnarled hand and I took it. "Nice of you to visit an old man," he said with a smile. "I sure used up a lot of adjectives on you in the old days."

"Some of them weren't very nice."

"Company policy," he laughed. "You always made a great bad guy. But how the hell did you always come out clean?"

"That's my policy," I said.

He came around the counter lighting the stub of a chewed cigar. "You got it made, Mike. Now, what can I do for you?"

"Mitch Temple was in the other day. . . ."

He coughed in the cigar smoke and regarded me with amazement. "You're in this?"

"Sideways. Can you keep it quiet?"

"Sure. I'm not on a beat."

I gave him a quick picture of my meeting with Mitch Temple and the possibility that his death might be involved in something I was working on. Biff knew I wasn't putting it all on the line but it was to be expected and he didn't mind. Let him alone and he'd put some of the pieces together himself.

Biff said, "All I can do is tell you what I told the others. Mitch came down and spent a while here going through the files. I was busy at the desk and didn't pay any attention to him. He didn't ask for anything and didn't check anything out."

"His column doesn't often carry photographs."

"That's right. When it did they were usually new ones supplied by some press agent. Then they were filed away down here."

"What section was he working in?"

"Hell, Mike, I can't see beyond that first tier. He was out of sight all the time. All the rest asked me that same question. I could hear him banging drawers, but that was all."

"Anybody else come in while he was here?"

Biff thought a moment, then said, "I know where he wasn't. All the show-biz and Broadway files are on the left there. He was back in the general news section, but they're cross-indexed alphabetically, by occupation and a few other headings. Hell, Mike, Al Casey who does the feature crime yarns even dusted around for Mitch's prints on the cabinets and didn't come up with anything. I don't know where he was poking around."

I didn't pay any attention to the other old guy

in the coveralls who was pushing a broom around the floor until he said, "I sure know where he was."

Both of us turned around slowly and looked at him. He never stopped his sweeping. My voice came out in a hoarse whisper. "Where?"

"The P-T section. He left all the damn butts squashed out on the floor and I had to scrape 'em up."

"Why didn't you say something?" Biff said.

"Nobody asked me," he growled.

I said, "Show me," and Biff led me back around the floor-to-ceiling rows of files until we came to the section between P and T.

Then all we did was stand there. There were forty separate drawers in the section, each a good four feet deep and crammed with folders. Biff said, "You know how many items are in this place?" I shook my head. "Figure at least a hundred to the drawer and each folder with at least ten photographs. You got a lot of looking to do, friend. Maybe you can suggest something."

"How do you get to the top drawers?"

"There's a stepladder down the end."

I waved for Biff to follow me and found the old guy emptying his sweepings into a trash can. "Did Mitch Temple have that ladder out when he was here?"

"Yep." He spit into the can, slid the top on and walked away.

"I know," Biff muttered, "nobody asked him. Now what?"

"Half of those files are eliminated. If Al Casey has the time he might try working over the other half."

"If I know him, he'll make the time," Biff said.

"Just do me a favor, keep me out of it," I told him.

Biff's face twisted into a puzzled expression. "You mean I'm supposed to have had the idea?"

"You've had them before, haven't you?"

"That was before."

"Well, you got one again."

I grabbed a cruising cab on Forty-second Street and had him take me back to the Hackard Building. The working crowd had cleared out an hour ago and the city was going through its momentary lull while the night closed in around it. I took the elevator up to the eighth floor and walked down the corridor to my office, my heels echoing hollowly in the empty space.

My keys were in my hand, but I didn't put them in the lock. Tacked to the frame was a white sheet of paper that covered one of the panes of frosted glass with the simple typewritten note, *Back Later*, across it.

I slid the .45 out of the sling, thumbed the safety off and the hammer back and moved so my shadow wouldn't fall across the door. I had had other notes stuck on my door, but this one had been written on my own brand of bonded paper in the brown typing we always used and had to come from inside the room. Only it was something neither Velda nor I would have done.

84

I reached over and pulled the paper away. There was a fist-sized hole in the pane right by the lock that a glass cutter had made and the note was tacked over it so nobody would notice it and possibly report it downstairs.

They didn't even bother to lock up after they had left. The knob turned under my hand and I shoved the door open. I reached in, flicked the light on, then walked inside and kicked the door shut with my foot.

Somebody had been very neat about it. Thorough, but neat. The place had been given a professional shakedown from one end to the other and not one thing had been missed. The desk drawers and cabinets had been emptied, but their contents were in inverted piles, systematically scrutinized and left lying there. Nobody ripped up seat cushions any more, but each one had been turned over and inspected for signs of fresh stitching and all the furniture had been pulled out to see if anything had been concealed behind it.

Now it was getting interesting. Somewhere out there in the maw of the city somebody was concerned about my participation in something. I sat down in my chair, swung around and looked out at the lights that outlined New York.

The possibilities were limited. To somebody, the fact that I was the one to find the Delaney girl could have seemed like more than a coincidence. With her background, she could have been involved in something heavy enough to warrant investigation from private sources and I was on her tail.

Or was it Greta Service? The prison grapevine could have passed along Harry's concern about his sister's absence and his contact with me and if Greta had been wrapped up with the wrong people, they wouldn't want me poking around.

Then there was Mitch Temple. A guy like that could always pop an exposé that was worth a kill if it could be kept quiet.

Somebody wanted to know how much I knew. Somebody didn't know I knew about the thread that tied all three of those people together.

I picked up the phone and dialed Velda's apartment. After four rings her service answered and when I identified myself, said she hadn't called in since that afternoon. I left a message for her to contact me at the usual places and hung up.

There was no sense dusting the place down for prints; a pro would have worn gloves anyway. Nothing was missing as far as I could see and the data Velda had compiled for me would be in the safe at Lakland's — a precaution we always took.

I used a piece of cardboard and covered the hole in the glass from the inside, then snapped the lock, walked out and closed the door.

Silence has a funny sound. You hear it in the jungles when everything is too still and you know there's somebody in the trees with a gun ready to pick you off. You hear it in a crowded room when everybody turns off the conversation when you walk in the door and you know the hostile element is ready and waiting.

I could hear it in the corridor and before the parrots could scream with indignation of sudden movement and the monkeys jump with alarm at shattering blasts, I hit the floor and rolled, the .45 in my hand spitting back at the half-opened door behind me where the guy in the black suit was trying to bring me into the sights of his automatic and getting nowhere because his bullets were tearing aimlessly into the tile and ricocheting off the walls while mine had already punched three holes into his chest.

chapter five

He lay face down in the half-opened doorway, death so new that it hadn't erased the look of surprise on his face. I nudged the door open, flipped the light switch with the tip of my finger and looked around the room. There was nothing fancy about the Hackard Building or the offices it rented. This one was a minimum setup with a wooden desk, a pair of chairs and a coat rack. A layer of dust was spread evenly over everything, the window was grimy and the floor scuffed and splintered from the countless pieces of equipment that had been moved in and out.

The guy had drawn up a chair close to the door to be able to listen to any activity in the hall outside. Chances were that he had shaken my place down, found nothing and waited for me. If the door had opened from the other side he would have had a clear shot at my back before I could have done anything about it and Pat would have had me in his statistical columns instead of his address book.

I went through his pockets, found sixty-two bucks and some change, a pair of rubber gloves you could buy anywhere and two fairly stiff plastic strips that I slipped into my own pocket.

None of his clothes were new. His suit had come from a large chain and looked about a year old, matching everything else. Unless the police had a record on the guy, or could come up with something out of the lab, getting a make on him wasn't going to be easy. He looked to be in his late forties, on the thin side and about five ten or so. His dark hair had receded, but there was no gray showing, so my guess at his age could have been off. I studied his face again, taking in the sharp features and the odd skin coloration. There was a death pallor there but it couldn't obliterate some of the characteristics common to some Europeans or Latin Americans.

One thing was sure, it wasn't a plain contract kill. Those guys specialize in one field and don't bother with any shakedown job to boot. Either there were two involved or this one was on assignment to find out what I knew or make sure I didn't find out any more.

But what the hell had I found out?

I stepped over the body and went back into the corridor. The elevator was still where it had left me and nobody had come to investigate the shots. It wasn't strange. The old building was solidly built and could muffle noise almost completely.

There was still a way to play it. I'd be asking for trouble, but it would keep me from doing too much explaining and it was simple enough to look right. Three of the offices down the hall from mine were occupied by small businesses that could conceivably keep something of value on the premises. In the door of each one, I knocked a hole in the glass panes, reached in and opened the lock, hoping none of them had alarms wired to them. Every room got the same treatment, a little disturbance that would indicate a search and the rubber gloves in the guy's pocket would explain the lack of prints. In the last place there was a gold wrist watch lying on top of a desk and I took it out and dropped it in the dead man's pocket for a clincher.

Then I went back to my own office and called Pat.

By nine-thirty they had bought my story. The guy at the newsstand downstairs had remembered the guy coming in after everybody had left and as he was closing up. Two of the men who rented the other offices said they did a cash business, but never left money in the office overnight, but for someone who didn't know it, they were probably targets for a robbery. The watch in the corpse's pocket made the deal firm. My version was that I had seen the broken windows, checked my own office and started out to see if anyone was still around when he tried to nail me. The manager admitted that a lot of the empty offices were unlocked, so the probability was that the guy had heard the elevator coming up, slipped into one to hide, and when he started out to make a getaway, saw me, panicked and started shooting.

I knew better. He had come prepared to

handle a lock with those plastic strips. My door wouldn't give in to that technique so he had broken the window, but they made it easy for him to wait me out in a convenient empty office.

Pat drove me downtown and took my statement there. Before I finished, one of the detectives came in and told him there was no make on the guy yet, but that the gun was a .38 Colt Cobra licensed to a jeweler that had been stolen in a robbery two months before. The lab hadn't come up with any laundry marks on the guy's clothes and the only lead they had was that he had been wearing shoes made and sold in Spain but they were probably as old as his clothes. His prints had been wired to Washington and pictures were telephotoed to Interpol in case he was a foreign national.

Pat took my statement, read it through once and tossed it on his desk. "I almost believe it," he said. "Damn it, I almost believe it."

"You're a spooky slob," I grunted.

"I'm supposed to be, buddy. Right now I'm spooked more than ever. First the Delaney thing, now this."

"At least this one's cut and dry."

"Is it?" he asked softly.

"Nobody's looking for your scalp."

He interlocked his fingers and smiled at me, his eyes cold. "Are they looking for *yours*, Mike?"

I smiled back at him. "They'll have a hard time getting it."

"Don't con me."

"You have statements from five witnesses besides me that put a common robbery motive behind this, a stolen gun, gloves, a paraffin test that shows he shot at me, the position of the corpse proving concealment, so what more do you want?"

"I could tell you another way things *might* have been arranged," Pat said. "The only reason I'm not hammering at it is because the manager's statement is the only one that sticks with me . . . the fact he admitted that occasionally some empty offices are left unlocked. There was one other open one on your floor, but the rest were locked."

"Okay, I was lucky. I was there with a gun. Anybody else would have been written off and you'd have an unsolved one on your hands."

"We're not done with this one yet, you know."

"I hope not. I'd like to know who he was myself."

"You'll find out. Think it might tie into something you're on?"

I got up and stretched, then slapped on my hat. "The only thing I'm on is trying to locate Greta Service."

"Maybe I can help you on that." He reached in his desk drawer, took out an envelope and handed it to me. "Authorization to see old Harry. Your conversation will be recorded. Tomorrow you'll probably hear from the D.A. on your court appearance. Don't stay away too long."

"Thanks, chum."

"No trouble. You interest me. I always wonder how far you'll get before you wind up with your ass in a sling."

On some people prison life had a therapeutic effect. Harry Service was one of them. He had slimmed down and his face had lost the hostility it had worn at the trial and he was genuinely glad to see me. There was a momentary surprise, but he knew all the tricks and expected that I did too and anything taken down on tape for analysis later wasn't going to add up any hard points for him.

I said, "See your sister lately?"

"Nope. She sure knows how to worry a guy."

"She's big enough to take care of herself."

"That I wouldn't mind. What bugs me is she wants to take care of me too. I tried to tell her I'd make out. . . . After this stretch I'm going legit, believe me."

"Well," I said, "I wish I could tell you something, but I couldn't locate her. She moved from her last place. One of her friends saw her uptown once, but that was the end of it. I wouldn't sweat it if I were you."

"You ain't me though, Mike. She's all I got for family."

"Maybe you know some of her friends."

He looked at me meaningfully. "Not any more."

"Yeah," I said. "Tell me . . . what was she like when she visited you last?"

Harry squirmed in his seat and frowned. "Well, she was . . . well, different."

"How?"

"I don't know how to say it. She wouldn't tell me nothing. She said pretty soon everything was going to be all right because she was going to get a lot of dough. I didn't think about it much because that's what she said right along. This time, though, she wouldn't say how. Like it was a big secret. The part I don't like is that her face was the way she looked as a kid when she done something she shouldn't of."

"Did she mention any of her former . . . friends?" I asked him.

"That was before the last time," Harry said. "Something was cooking and she didn't say, but I caught on that they all might have part of the action. Funny thing, Greta wasn't one what makes friends fast. The ones she usually took to were kind of oddballs, sort of misplaced types."

"Mixed up?" I suggested.

Harry shook his head. "No, not that. Kind of don't-give-a-damn people. I think that was why she stayed in the Village."

"You're not much help," I said.

"I know," Harry nodded. "Only thing I could put my finger on was when she was here last she opened her pocketbook and I saw a letter in there that was postmarked . . ." He paused, and wrote with his forefinger on the countertop, *Bradbury.* "I remembered it because I almost pulled a job there once," he said. "Then, when I

94

mentioned it to her she snapped the pocketbook shut and said it wasn't nothing at all and I knew damn well she was lying."

"You mean out on the Island?"

"That's the place." He ran his tongue over his lips and added as an afterthought, "Something else . . . that letter was light green, kind of. It was long, like a business would use."

I looked at my watch. The time was almost up. "Okay, kid, I'll see what I can do."

"You'll try real hard, okay, Mike?"

"The best I can."

Harry stood up and looked at me anxiously. "And Mike . . . I ain't got no hard feelings about being in here. It's my own fault. I'm just glad I didn't shoot you."

"You're luckier than most, Harry," I told him, but he hadn't heard about last night and didn't get the meaning at all.

On the way back to the city I picked up a news-paper at a gas stop and flipped through the pages. All the local news was obscured by the latest trouble spot in the world and the state-ments from the U.N. idiots who fostered the whole mess and were trying to explain their way out of it. Right now they were trying to make the United States the goat again and we were falling for it. I spit out the window in disgust and read the small blurb that detailed the shooting in the Hackard Building. Space was so limited that they didn't bother going into my background again except to mention that I was the one who had discovered the Delaney girl's body. The story simply stated that I had interrupted a burglar and killed him when he tried to shoot his way past me. So far the dead man had not been identified.

Velda and Hy Gardner were having coffee in the office when I got there. They sat on opposite sides of the room making small talk, deliberately avoiding the big thing that was on their minds. The place seemed charged with some unseen force that oozed from both of them.

Hy took the cigar out of his mouth and said, "Well, you did it again."

I tossed my hat on the rack. "Now what?"

Something like a look of relief passed over Velda's face. "You could have let me know where you were."

"What's everybody worried about me for?"

"Mike . . ." Hy drained his cup and put it on the desk. "Pat's sitting on this latest bit of yours. You think we don't know it? It was a good story, friend, but we all know better."

Velda said, "The D.A. called. You have a court appearance this Monday. He's after your license."

"So what else is new?"

She grinned and poured me a cup of coffee. "Ask Hy."

I looked over at him. "Got something?"

"Something you started. Old Biff down at the morgue got Al Casey back and they pulled about thirty folders Mitch handled when he was poking around in the morgue. They catalogued the photos Mitch handled and it's the damndest conglomeration you ever saw, from polo players to politicians. Right now he thinks you know more than you're telling and they want you to see what Mitch was looking for."

"Biff said he didn't check anything out."

"Hell, Mike, he could have stuck it in his pocket if he had wanted to."

"What for? If he was looking for an I.D. on somebody he would have gotten it right there."

Hy scrutinized my face closely. "Do you know what it was?"

"No," I said simply.

"Then why did somebody try to kill you?"

"I don't know that, either."

For a few seconds Hy was silent, then he nodded and stuck the cigar back in his mouth and stood up. "All right, I'll go for it." He pulled a manila envelope out of his pocket and flipped it on the desk. "The copies of Greta Service's photos you asked for. I passed the rest out. The gang will keep their eyes open."

"Thanks, Hy."

He picked up his coat, headed toward the door and stopped beside me. "Just tell me one thing off the record to satisfy my curiosity. That guy you shot . . . it didn't happen like you told it, did it?"

I grinned at him and shook my head. "No."

"Damn," he said and walked out.

Velda locked the door behind him and went back to her desk. "It's pretty deep, isn't it?"

97

"We're on something. It's not tangible, but it's got somebody worried all to hell." I briefed her on my conversation with Harry Service and the details of the gunfight in the corridor, watching her face furrow with concern.

"I asked around the neighbors where Helen Poston lived. A few of them were able to describe a friend of hers that tallied with Greta. One old biddy turned out to be a people-watcher who drew a lot of her own conclusions, but the main thing she brought out was that Helen Poston was neither happy nor doing too well until after she met Greta. From then on she started turning up in new clothes and staying away from the house on weekends. Greta had a car the woman couldn't identify and on Friday nights they'd leave, Helen with a suitcase, and get back sometime Monday. One night she didn't come back at all and that's when she was found dead."

"That's the first I heard about a car," I said.

"Rented, probably. A kid described it as a black compact with no trim, so we can assume it was an agency vehicle. You want me to check with the garages that handle them?"

"Yeah . . . and get the mileage records. Did Greta — or whoever it was — show up after the Poston kid died?"

"Apparently not. There was a police investigation and her parents picked up her clothes. Three days later her room was rented to somebody else."

"Anybody else asking around there?"

"Not as far as I could find out. I played it cool enough so nobody would identify me again in case you're worried."

"I'm worried," I told her. "From now on we'll stay away from the office. You take a room at the Carter-Layland Hotel and get me one adjoining. . . ."

"Oh boy," she grinned.

I faked a swing at her and she faked ducking. I looked at my watch. It was three-thirty. "Let's cut," I said.

Pat had identified the guy who tried to kill me. We sat at one end of the bar in the Blue Ribbon having a sandwich and beer before the supper crowd came in and he let me scan the report that had gotten to his office an hour before.

Interpol, through their Paris office, had picked his prints and mug shots out of their files and transferred them to New York immediately. His name had been Orslo Bucher, accredited with Algerian citizenship, an army deserter and minor criminal with three convictions. He had escaped from a prison camp three years ago and been unheard from since. The report said there was no present evidence of him having applied for a passport from any country they serviced.

"Illegal entry," I suggested.

"We get a few hundred every year. There are probably thousands in the country we don't know about. A lot of the traffic comes up through Mexico and the Gulf coastline."

"Why here, Pat?"

He said, "The Washington Bureau thinks it's because they want political sanctuary. They have enemies in other countries. Because of their criminal records they can't come in legally."

"And this one?"

Pat shrugged and took a bite of his sandwich. "Who knows? We traced him to a room in the Bronx he had occupied for a year and a half. He did odd jobs, seemed to have enough money to keep him going, though nothing fancy, and didn't cultivate any friends except for a couple of jokers at the neighborhood bar. He serviced a whore every two weeks or so without any unnecessary conversation. The only thing she remembered was that the last time around he made her change a fifty instead of giving it to her in the assorted bills he usually did."

"New money?" I asked him.

He got the point. "If he had any more, we didn't find it. I'd figure that if you were the target for a contract kill it would go higher than what he was showing and the gun hand would have had a little more class. That's why I'm still letting your story stand, old buddy."

I grinned at him and hoisted the beer. "He was an army type and that pistol he carried wasn't a zip gun."

"Hell, I figured that, but who isn't ex-military any more? And with his background you could expect him to tote a little hardware. It isn't that hard to come by." He paused and put down his sandwich. "Incidentally, we found some burglar tools and some goodies lifted in a previous robbery in his room,"

I kept my face straight and nodded. Pat was really scrambling it now. He was throwing the possibility that the guy really had tried to knock off my office for something of monetary value instead of having either Velda or me as a primary target and all I did was add to the picture by phonying the other break-ins.

"And now the case is closed," I said.

Pat washed his last bite down and shoved the glass back. His eyes went over my face and the lines that played with the corners of his mouth weren't a smile. "Is it?" he asked me.

When a few seconds went by, I said, "Don't nudge me, Pat."

"Last night we exhumed a body. It was that of a young girl supposedly killed in a car crash about four months ago. She was burned beyond recognition, but we got a make from a routine inquiry on her dental work a month later. The lab reports said she was loaded to the gills, and that quite literally. Anybody with the alcohol content she had shouldn't have been able to drive at all. However, making exceptions for certain tolerances people show, we had to assume that's what caused it. She was known as a heavy drinker and a wild kid who could really hold the stuff. She was last seen alive in a slop chute in the Village and said she was going on a party somewhere without saying anything more. The ones she was with were well alibied and told us it was nothing new. She took off in her car and what happened wasn't totally unexpected."

"Then what's your angle, Pat?"

"A more detailed autopsy showed injuries not normally sustained in a car crash, even one of that magnitude. Even the heat couldn't account for certain aspects of her condition."

"You're not saying much, kiddo."

"Ever hear of the rack?"

"Come off it, Pat!"

"Nasty thought," he said, "but look at this." He held out a photo and let me look at it. It was a reduced studio picture of a lovely, well-built girl in her middle twenties, swathed in a sheer, Grecian-style dress, posed languidly against an artificial column, a seductive expression in her dark eyes and the trace of a smile creasing her mouth.

"What about her?"

"Registered with the police department as a night-club entertainer. Good appearance, but a lousy voice so she didn't make out. Her agent couldn't sell her except as a hostess in a few joints and said she picked up money from the johns in the places she worked and seemed to do all right. Orphaned at sixteen with a crippled brother in Des Moines who drew a full World War Two disability pension and ran a moderately prosperous market on the side. He sent the money to bury her."

He gave me another long, steady look. "Tie in the others and what do you have?"

"Somebody loves nice bodies," I said.

"There's one other thing."

"So?"

"This one knew Greta Service," Pat said. "They both worked for the same two outfits in the garment district at the same time, modeling identical lines. Phil Silvester photographed them together for their brochure."

"Got a pick-up out on her?"

"In five states." He paused and glanced at me out of the corners of his eyes. "We covered some of your ground but didn't get too much cooperation. How did you make out?"

"No better."

"Harry Service wouldn't talk, either."

"Put him in jail," I said.

"Quit trying to be funny, Mike. He mentioned a letter to you without giving the postmark. The tape was clear at that point."

"He didn't say," I told him.

"Withholding evidence isn't a pretty matter, chum."

"Evidence of what? All I have is privileged information. I'm working for Harry, remember?"

"Balls." Pat's face grew tight. "I'm not going to play you down, Mike. Right now I want an opinion. Do you think there's any tie-in between these women?"

I waved to Ed to bring me another beer and finished half of it before I answered him. "Look, Pat . . . we have three kids in allied professions. It's possible they all knew each other. It's a damn tight business so it's likely they ran into each other. Let's assume they did. Two are dead and one is missing."

"You forgot the fourth one."

"For the moment that's pure speculation. Check your statistics and you'll see how many die every hour."

"Think maybe Greta Service is dead?"

"No. A friend of hers saw her alive and not too far from here not long ago."

"Mike, they were show kids, no family ties and not in the big time. Any of them would hustle for a buck."

"And you and I know plenty like that. You're angling for the Jack-the-Ripper bit, aren't you?"

"It's possible. There's a curious part to it. None of those girls were sexually molested prior to their deaths."

"If it's one man he's got a damn good operation going. Just tell me this . . . and it's your thought . . . why go so far out for a remote poison to knock off the Poston girl? How would he have access to the stuff if it's that scarce? It doesn't fit the pattern."

"But there's a pattern," Pat insisted.

"Sure, if you look at it like that."

Pat swung around and looked straight at me. "Which brings us straight back to you, friend."

"Now you're sweating me."

"Nope. That'll come later, old pal. Right now I'm just wondering about one thing. That business with Orslo Bucher. Did it happen the way you said it did?"

"Funny, Hy asked me the same thing."

"What did you tell him?"

"Does Macy's tell Gimbel's?"

Pat threw his half of the lunch money on the bar top. "Don't get too deep, Mike. You don't go solo in this world very long. We've played a lot of games together. Let's not quit here. I know how you think, so I'm going along with you for now, but remember that upstairs, people are after your neck. If you fall, I can too, so stay loose."

"I'm so loose I jingle."

"Just one more time. For me. And off the record. The bit with Bucher . . . *did* it happen like that?"

I shook my head. "Nope."

"You know what you are, don't you?"

"I've been told often enough," I said.

Orslo Bucher's neighborhood wasn't new to me. It lay in the fringe area adjoining a slum section that was marked for urban renewal when they could figure out where to put the people that were already there. You could feel the depression that hung over the buildings like an emotional smog, see it in the gray wash that dangled from the clotheslines between the buildings and in the restless hostility of the inhabitants. It was a place that existed on the gratuity of the city's Welfare Department, but the bars were filled and the curbs lined with an assortment of misused cars.

Two years ago we had mopped up a bunch

who had peddled home-made booze that had killed off fifteen people at a party, and there would still be some around who liked the feel of the cash I had laid out to get a line on the slobs. The police would get a few reluctant facts, a squeeze on their informers might get them a little more, but when they saw the long green and knew I wasn't submitting official reports they'd lay it out for me.

Max Hughes was the night bartender at the Seville, a grungy corner slop chute. He had just come on the shift when I walked in, mopped the bar top down with a dirty rag and gave me the barest glance of recognition. Without being asked, he slid a beer in front of me and changed the twenty I put down.

"Orslo Bucher," I said. I tapped the ten-spot on the counter and watched it disappear under his fingers.

He leaned forward, propping his elbows on the mahogany. "You the one who bumped him?"

I nodded.

"Thought it was you. Hell, he was asking for it."

"Why?"

"Petty crap. He was always pulling something."

"Alone?"

"Strictly," Max said. "Nobody much wanted him around anyway. Kind of a mean one. I tossed him out a couple of times when he was loaded and he looked like he wanted to kill me."

"He make any trouble around here?"

106

"No . . . but I'd lay odds he was the one pulled that armed stickup on Arnie's liquor store last month. I felt that iron he carried when I heaved him out."

"Who'd know about him, Max?"

"Like I said . . . nobody. He was either in his pad, one of the joints or gone. Nobody cared." Max squinted and rubbed his chin. "Funny thing though, once I seen him getting into a big new car over on Lenox Avenue. He got in the back and the car had a chauffeur. I didn't see who he was with, except the guy wore a homburg and seemed to know him. It wasn't the kind of company Bucher usually kept."

"Sure it was him?"

"Positive." He frowned again and tapped the back of my hand with his finger. "Come to think of it, old Greenie said he seen the same thing once. I didn't believe him because Greenie's bombed out on booze and can't think straight. He kept telling me it was a dipple car, whatever the hell that is, but he's always got a screwy name for everything."

"Suppose I talk to Greenie."

Max grunted and said, "You'll have to go six feet down to do it. He got clipped by a truck two months ago and died in Bellevue."

I was getting nowhere in a hurry. When Max couldn't supply any answers there weren't any to be had. I said, "What about that whore Bucher used?"

"Rosie? Man, that one's on the last time

around. She'll bang for a beer or a buck and lucky to get either. The only ones she gets is the bums the other hustlers won't touch. Lucy Digs and Dolly gave Bucher the brush when he tried to warm their pads, that's why he wound up with Rosie, and when them two turn anything down, it got to be pretty sad. Nope, old Bucher wasn't too popular around here. He ain't going to be missed none at all. Not none. If it wasn't for the cops nosing around nobody would have given him a thought."

"Okay, kid, if that's the best you can do."

"Sorry, Mike. That's the way it is. Suppose something turns up?"

I took out a card and wrote the name of the hotel on it. "Call me here if you think it's important." He looked up at me with shrewd eyes. "I'll mail you a check," I said.

Hy was just getting ready to leave his office when I reached him. He had been trying to get me for the past hour and was about to give up. Too many people were around for him to talk, so he told me to meet him at Teddy's place as fast as I could. I walked up a block, grabbed a cab and gave him the address of the restaurant in the lower end of Manhattan.

He was waiting for me in a private section and he wasn't alone. He pointed to a seat and indicated the tall lanky guy next to him. "You know Al Casey?"

"I've seen you around." I held out my hand and he took it. "Biff told me about you going over the morgue files. Come up with anything?"

"That's what we wanted to talk to you about," Hy said. "Sit down."

I pulled out a chair and he nodded to Al. "Fill him in."

Al eased back in his chair and had a sip of his coffee. "First, we think we found Mitch Temple's last contact. He was in a woman's clothing shop on Broadway asking about those damn negligees and finally bought one. He had given his name and the office address to the salesgirl and laid down twenty bucks for a twelve-dollar item. The girl left to ring up the sale and when she came back he was gone. Now on Broadway, people don't just leave tips like that, so the girl remembered the incident after a little bit of persuasion. She hadn't mentioned it before because she didn't want the manager to know she had taken any cash on the side. The second thing she remembered was that while she was writing up the sales slip, Mitch kept looking at another customer down further in the store who was poking around a clothes rack and was preoccupied enough so that she had to ask him twice about the address before he gave it to her. She never saw either one again."

"What did Mitch buy?"

"A black nylon shortie outfit. Real sexy, she said. What we figure is, he recognized the other guy and followed him out. The date on the sales slip tallies with the day he first started to go through the morgue files."

"Anybody else recognize the other one?"

"No. There was one new girl who might have waited on him, but apparently he didn't buy anything. If it was the one she *thought* she remembered, it was just a man who asked if that were all the colors they had in stock. She said that was it and he left. What was peculiar about it . . . there was a complete color assortment of new stock that had just been put out that morning."

I looked at the two of them and felt my mind fingering out the bits and pieces until there was only one little piece left.

"Complete except for one," I said.

Al Casey shook his head. "Every color. I even checked their stock records."

"Not white," I told him.

Both of them looked at each other and a frown began to form between Al's eyes. "That's right," he said. "There wasn't any white. But how would you know?"

"Mitch Temple told me. That's why he was reaching for that white handkerchief in his pocket. Not for anything else he had."

Hy shoved his glasses up on his forehead and stared at me hard. "I don't get it, Mike."

"Velda spotted it first," I told him. "Green for redheads, black for blondes. What color dame would look best in white?"

After a moment Hy said, "A brunette or black-haired doll."

"Like Greta Service," I added.

chapter six

There was a pattern coming out now. All it took was for that first piece to fall in place. Pat might have put his finger on it after all. Police records were spotted with psycho types who would go to any extremes to satisfy their own strange desires. They could be as devious as a snake and harder to track down. They could weave their own schemes into such fantastically intricate designs that there seemed to be no beginning nor end of the confusion. It wasn't so much a pattern as a suggestion of one, but it was there.

I said, "How much of this has Pat got?"

"His own squad made the same rounds. If they got different answers that's their tough luck."

"How long do you expect to sit on it?"

"Until we get one step further," Al told me. "Norm Harrison got back from Washington today where he was covering the latest Senate subcommittee investigations. He was going to go through all his papers to see if Mitch dropped a note to him after he couldn't reach him by phone. There was a mail chute in Mitch's apartment house, so it's a possibility."

Hy lit his cigar and blew the match out through a cloud of smoke. "I'm going to see him tonight. He's covering a political bash one of the U.N. members is giving for a newly admitted country. One of those splinter groups from Africa we're supporting. You want to go along?"

"Why me?"

"Because you're in this as deep as we are and damn well know it. We're not passing up any chance of missing an angle on Mitch's death even if we have to play along with you."

"Thanks, pal," I grinned. I looked at Al Casey. "And you?"

"Back to those files. I think I know the system Mitch used in going through them. It wasn't alphabetical. If I can find the last folder he hit we'll narrow it down pretty well. Even if something's missing, we can check it against the negative files."

I pushed back from the table and got up. "Okay, buddy, I'm with you."

The town house of Gerald Ute was a newly restored three-story building just off Fifth Avenue opposite Central Park. My own knowledge of Ute came from sketchy newspaper accounts and on the way over Hy briefed me on his background. He owned several flourishing corporations that had expanded into the multimillion-dollar class since 1950, but he himself hadn't erupted onto the social scene until his wife decided Chicago was too restrictive for their new position and coerced him into a move to New York. She lasted a year before she made him a widower, but Ute had gotten to enjoy the high life of society circles he could afford and he widened his activities so that he was everything from patron of obscure arts to unofficial host to visiting dignitaries.

Apparently Ute was smart enough to stay out of the political jungle, though on several occasions his influence was used to mollify ruffled feathers among the U.N. members he cultivated. His activities didn't seem to interfere with his businesses, which were still climbing on the big board in the Stock Exchange, and at sixty-two, he was pretty well out of the scandal class.

The muted sounds of a string quartet floated through the rooms against the background of quiet murmuring. A butler took our hats and behind him the guests were gathering in small groups, waiters circulating with trays of champagne glasses. There was little formality. Most of the men were in business suits, a few in black ties, while the women fed their vanities in Paris originals winking with diamonds.

Gerald Ute knew the value of good public relations. I saw Richie Salisbury who usually covered the Washington beat, Paul Gregory whose "Political Observations" were featured in a national magazine and Jean Singleton who usually handled the foreign news coverage. Ute was talking to Norman Harrison when we walked in, stopped long enough to come over and say hello to Hy and be introduced to me.

For all of his years, he was still ruggedly handsome, though starting to bulge out at the middle. He had the sharp eyes of the shrewd speculator that could laugh at locker-room jokes or cut ice if they had to. When they focused on mine they were reading me like a computer being programmed and he said, "Mr. Hammer. Yes, you've made some headlines recently."

"Accidentally," I said.

"But good for business." He dropped my hand and smiled.

"Sometimes."

"It's too bad I can't write half the things I know about him," Hy put in.

"Why don't you?"

Hy let out a laugh. "Because Mike might decide to write a biography and I'd be in it. How's the party going?"

"Fine, fine. It's just a welcoming thing for Naku Em Abor and his party . . . getting him acquainted with the city and all that. People will be drifting in and out all evening. Suppose I introduce you around."

Hy waved him off. "Don't bother. I know everybody anyway. If I don't, I will."

"And you, Mr. Hammer?"

Before I could answer Hy said, "Don't worry about him, Gerald. You never know who this guy is buddies with."

"Then let me introduce you to our hostess for the evening." He walked between us to the nearest couple, a woman in a black strapless gown that flowed over her body like a silvery fluid who was talking to a small oriental in a tuxedo. He said, "My dear . . . if you have a moment . . ."

She turned around, her hair still glinting like a halo, eyes twinkling and touched so that they seemed to turn up at the corners, and when they looked at me, widened with pleasure and Dulcie McInnes said, "Why, Mike, how nice to see you here!"

Hy nudged Gerald Ute with his elbow and whispered, "See what I mean?"

Our host laughed, presented James Lusong, talked for a few moments, then the three of them went back to the others, leaving me with Dulcie and a glass of champagne.

"From fashion editor to hostess," I said.

"Our advertisers appreciate the association." She took my arm and steered me through the crowd, nodding to friends and occasionally introducing me. I saw Hy to one side speaking quietly to Norm Harrison, but couldn't overhear what they were saying. "It adds class to our publications," Dulcie told me.

"It won't if you're seen with me," I said.

"Ah, but you add excitement. Society girl on safari with white hunter."

"That doesn't make for healthy relationships."

Her fingers squeezed my arm and she grinned up at me. "No, but interesting ones. After you left the office there were all sorts of speculation going on. I rather thought our employees read only the more gentle periodicals, then I find they like sensationalism too. You seem to have supplied it for them. A few discreet questions and I learned a lot about you."

"I'm surprised you'll still speak to me, Miss McInnes."

"You know women better than that," she said. "And the name is Dulcie. Now . . . satisfy my curiosity. . . . Since you weren't on the guest list, how did you make it here?"

"Power of the press. Friend Hy Gardner was invited and dragged me along. Not that I'm much on these bashes, but we have an appointment later."

"Any friend of the press is a friend of Gerald's. I'm glad you made it. Anyone here you'd like to meet?"

In four different spots around the room, men were clustered in a tight circle, laughing occasionally, talking with that odd intensity they developed when the nucleus of the circle was a pretty woman. "Maybe the Proctor Girls," I suggested.

Dulcie poked me with her finger. "Uh-uh. They're just eyewash. Besides, they're too young for you."

"How about them?" I indicated the men around the girls. Not one of them would ever see fifty again.

She looked at them and laughed lightly. "Funny, isn't it? When the Assembly is in session they're at each other's throats or thinking up some scheme to transform the world. Now here

116

they are simpering at twenty-year-olds like schoolboys. There's nothing like a pretty face to keep peace and quiet at a party."

"You ought to try it at the U.N. Maybe that's what they need."

"Oh, I've given it a thought. Gerald didn't exactly favor the idea the first time, but the Proctor Girls were such an asset he insists we invite them. Actually, it was his wife's idea originally."

"How did you get involved with being his hostess?"

"I'm a social climber, or haven't you heard?"

"Rumors," I admitted. "I'm not a member of the set myself."

"Fact is, I was born to this sort of thing. My family was Midwestern blue book and all that, I attended the right schools and made the proper friends, so that all of this comes naturally. I rather enjoy it." She sipped her champagne thoughtfully and said, "Every one of those Proctor Girls you see are from important families. One is engaged to a junior congressman, one to the son of a wealthy industrialist and the other two are being signed by a Hollywood studio."

"Lucky."

"No . . . they work for it. The qualifications for a Proctor Girl are quite rigorous. If they weren't, we couldn't afford to have them here." She put her empty glass on the tray of a passing waiter and took another. "By the way . . . have you found the girl you were looking for?"

"Not yet. It's a big city and it's easy to get buried in it. I'm giving it a little more time."

"Did the photographs help at all?"

I shrugged and shook my head. "Nobody's seen her. But you don't forget a face like that."

Dulcie turned and cocked her head, her eyes thoughtful. "You know, I'm wondering. . . ."

"What?"

"Teddy Gates . . . the one who photographed the girl you wanted. He has contracts independent of ours and sometimes uses models we turn down. It could be possible he kept a listing on her. He's done it before."

I could feel my neck muscles tighten with the thought of the possibility. "How can I reach him?"

"You won't have to. He keeps an office in our building and I have the keys." She looked at her watch and said, "It's eight now. We'll be breaking up here about midnight. Are you intending to stay?"

"No."

"Then suppose you meet me in the lobby of my building . . . say at twelve-thirty. We'll take a look."

"You don't mind?"

"Uh-uh. I like white hunters. Now let me go play hostess. Have fun."

I watched her walk away, appreciating the patrician stride that was so full of purpose, yet so totally feminine. Other eyes caught her as she passed, and watched regretfully when she was out of sight.

Norm Harrison hadn't found any communication from Mitch Temple. He had gone through his files and his notes without seeing even an interoffice memo. The kid who did his desk work said he remembered Mitch trying to contact him, but his conversation was hurried and the main point was for Norm to call him back when he came in. The kid didn't remember anything else.

We were all together in the library trying to figure out Mitch's reason for the call, but Norm couldn't put his finger on it and all he could speculate on was the one time they had been together at a party was when Mitch queried him about the political repercussions of his series on the Mafia. Since then Norm had been assigned to cover the general political situations in the U.N. and the forthcoming elections in the States, neither of which touched Mitch's area of operation.

One of the maids came in, told Hy he was wanted on the phone and we waited while he took the call. When he came back he had a look of excitement on his face, waited until we were alone and said, "Al Casey located the cabbie he thinks picked up Mitch. He had him follow another cab and passenger to a store on Twenty-first Street. They waited outside for about fifteen minutes, then this man came out with a package under his arm, walked to the end of the block and got into a private car he apparently had called for. They tailed him out to the Belt

Parkway, but the other car was going like hell and when the cabbie tried to keep it in sight, he got stopped by a police cruiser and picked up a ticket. Mitch had the guy drive him back uptown and got out near his apartment."

"He was sure it was Mitch?"

"The cabbie identified his photo. What made him remember was that Mitch tipped him enough to pay for the ticket."

"But no I.D. on the other car?" I asked.

"They never got close enough. It was getting dark, traffic was heavy and he said it was either a dark blue or black sedan. He didn't remember the make."

"How about the store?"

"None of the clerks were specific about the customers, but one did sell a white negligee that day. Al checked the sales slips. It was a cash purchase with no name or address."

I looked at Hy thoughtfully. Something was bugging me and I couldn't reach out and touch it. I said, "Pat better have this now."

"He's already got it," Hy said. "But what good's it going to do if we don't know who the hell we're looking for?"

"Mitch recognized him."

"And Mitch knew a hell of a lot of people."

"But why him?" I insisted. "What would make one guy stand out of a crowd buying sexy clothes for his doll?"

Norman said quietly, "Maybe he's done it before . . . been messed up in this sort of thing."

"We can find out," Hy told us. "Pat will be checking the M.O.'s and we can give him a hand. Want to come, Mike?"

"No, you go ahead. I'm going to try a different direction. I'll call you later."

Hy had that puzzled look back on his face again. "Look, Mike . . ."

"It's only an idea," I interrupted him. "We have to play this from all sides."

Gerald Ute seemed sorry to see us go, but wasn't insistent on our staying. We said good-by to a few of the others and Dulcie McInnes came over to walk us to the door. I told her something had come up I wanted to check on, but would see her at the Proctor Building as we planned.

Outside, Hy had flagged a cab, dropped me off opposite the News Building without asking any questions and went downtown. There was a small bar close by that the newspaper fraternity kept filled between shifts. Tim Riley was on his usual stool with his usual martini in his usual endless discussion of the New York Mets with the bartender. He was an old sports reporter assigned to the rewrite desk now, but he couldn't get baseball out of his system.

He gave me a big grin when I sat down next to him, but I didn't let him get started on the Mets. I said, "Favor time, Tim."

"Mike, I haven't got a ticket left. I . . ."

"Not that. It's about Mitch Temple."

He put his glass down, his face serious. "Anything. Just ask."

121

"Did he save carbons of his columns?"

Tim grimaced with his mouth and nodded. "Sure, they all do in case they need a reference later."

"I want to see them."

"You can go through back issues and . . ."

"That'll take too long. I'd sooner see his carbons."

He finished his drink with one swallow, pushed a bill across the bar and got off the stool. "Come on," he said.

Mitch Temple's cubicle of an office had the stale smell of disuse. An old raincoat still dangled from the hook behind the door and the ashtray was filled with snubbed butts. Somebody had gone through his drawers and left his papers stacked on his desk. Two three-drawer filing cabinets stood side by side, a couple of the drawers only partially closed, but since they only contained his original typewritten carbons stapled to their printed counterparts, there had been no thorough examination. Each folder contained his turnout for the month and they were dated back to two years ago. Some of the folders had cards clipped to their fronts cross-indexing Broadway items, rumors turning into fact, things of interest concerning personalities to be elaborated on later. I snagged the swivel chair with my toe, pulled it up in front of the files and sat down.

"Something I can help you with?" Tim asked me.

"I don't know what I'm looking for myself."

"Well, take your time. Nobody's going to bother you in here. And Mike . . . if you find anything, you yell, hear?"

"Don't worry, Tim. And thanks."

Mitch Temple had been more than an ordinary Broadway gossip columnist. Here and there little gems appeared that I remembered turning into cold, hard news stories later on. He had roved from one end of town to the other, Broadway his theme, but branching off into sidelines that turned him into a part-time crusader when he got hold of something. His series on the Mafia caused a full investigation of their activities with several convictions. Twice he got on politics and made a few faces red around town.

Dulcie McInnes and Gerald Ute appeared here and there when they either hosted a party or were guests at one. Some of Dulcie's escorts at society soireés were international figures in politics or finance. She was top-echelon jet set, traveling all over the world for the Proctor Group. Although Mitch reported her as being at different affairs of state and involved with pleasantries accorded the United Nations delegates, she didn't seem to show any political persuasion or be attached to anyone in particular.

Gerald Ute came in for a little closer coverage. He was always financing some far-out project or sounding off on things from scouting to the foreign problems. Twice, there was a romantic link to some prominent matron, but nothing came of it. In one column Mitch hinted that he had used his influence with the delegate of the deposed dictator of a South African nation to nail a fat mineral-rights contract for one of his companies, but in today's business arrangements, that's par for the course.

There were other names I recognized and others I didn't. For three consecutive weeks Mitch hammered at the hypocrisy of the United Nations regarding their commitments, naming Belar Ris, who had come out of obscurity after World War Two with a fortune behind him and had led an uprising that turned his country's colony into an independent nation that elected him their U.N. delegate. He was trying to force an acceptance of the part-Arabian complex headed by Naku Em Abor. Well, Mitch lost that one, I thought. The country was in and old Naku was being feted at Gerald Ute's party right now. Mitch tried a lot, but he didn't win them all. Despite his personal investigation and reporting of facts, two labor unions kept top hoods in office, an outlaw strike damn near destroyed the city and a leading politician was reelected even though he had a close affiliation with the Communist Party.

I had another ten minutes before I had to leave, so I took out the last of the folders in the drawer. They made interesting reading, but weren't at all informative. Belar Ris's name came up again, once when he got flattened by some playboy in a gin mill and once when the Italian government accused him of being associated with a group marketing black-market medicines for huge profits. There were a few other hot squibs about show-business personalities and some minor jabs at the present administration that weren't unusual.

About a third of Mitch's columns had been covered, and as far as I was concerned, it had been a waste of time. It had taken more than what he had written to cause him to be killed. Anybody with any common sense wouldn't want to tackle the entire newspaper staff and the police. And right there was the rub again. Supposing it wasn't someone with common sense . . . just a plain psychopath?

At twelve-twenty-five I was in the lobby of the Proctor Group Building getting a nervous look from a night watchman. Five minutes later Dulcie came in with a wave to both of us and he looked relieved to see her. Someplace she had changed to a skirt and sweater with a short coat thrown over her shoulders and she looked like a teen-ager out on a late date.

"Been here long?"

"Five minutes. Good party?"

"A social success. You left early or you would have met the great heads of great nations."

I said one word under my breath and she suppressed a giggle, her eyes laughing at me.

She had the key to a private elevator that whisked us up to the tenth floor, the area reserved for the photographers. She found the switch, threw the lights on and led me down the corridor past the vast film-developing and processing laboratory, the stages where the models were posed against exotic backdrops, down to the offices where we found the one labeled *Theodore Gates.*

"Here we are." She pushed the door open and stepped inside, turned the button on the desk lamp and walked to the cabinets along the wall. "Service, wasn't it?"

I nodded. "Greta Service."

She slid the drawer out, thumbed through a few envelopes and drew out one with Greta's name typed across the top. Inside were duplicate photos of the ones in the master file and a résumé of Greta's experience. The address was the one in Greenwich Village.

"No good," I said. "We'll need a later address."

She stuffed the folder back and shut the drawer. "Wait a minute." There was a rotary card file on Gates' desk and she flipped it around, stopped and said, "Could this be it?"

I looked at it. The notation listed her name, the Village number with a line drawn through it and another at the Sandelor Hotel, a fourth-rate fleabag on Eighth Avenue. A series of symbols at the bottom of the card may have been significant to Gates but didn't mean anything to me. In the bottom corner was another name, *Howell.*

"Well?"

"It's the only lead I got. I'm going to follow it up."

"Perhaps you could call first and . . ."

"No . . . I don't want to spook her off." I laid my hand over hers. "Thanks, kitten. I appreciate this."

There was a sad little expression in her eyes. "Would it be too much to ask . . . well, you *do* have me curious . . . can I go with you?"

I took her arm. "Sure, why not?"

We got out of the cab at the Sandelor Hotel and went into the lobby. It was a place for transients and permanent guests too impoverished or old to go any further. A musty smell of stale smoke and hidden decay hung in the air where it had been gathering for decades. The carpet was threadbare in front of the sagging cracked leather chairs, and in line to the desk and staircase. Drooping potted palms were spotted in the corners, two in front of the elevator that had an OUT OF ORDER sign on it.

The desk clerk was another relic, half asleep in a chair, three empty beer bottles beside him. I walked up and said, "You have a Greta Service here?"

He looked at me through half-opened eyes and shook his head. "Nobody by that name."

"You sure?"

"I said so, didn't I?"

Then I remembered the name on the bottom of the card and said, "How about Howell?"

He turned partly around, glanced at a chart pinned to the wall and nodded. "Second floor, two-oh-nine." He reached for the phone.

"Forget it," I told him.

For just a second he started to get irritated, then he took one hell of a good look at me, seemed to shrink back a little, made a motion with his shoulders and settled back into the chair. I took Dulcie's arm and steered her toward the stairs.

I knocked on the door twice before I heard a muffled sound from inside. When I knocked again a sleepy voice said, "All right, all right, don't knock the door down." I heard a chair being kicked, a soft curse, then a stripe of light showed under the door. The chain slid back, the lock clicked and the door swung open.

I said, "Hello, Greta."

It was her. It wasn't the Greta Service of the photographs, but it was her. Some of the beauty had eroded from her face, showing in the texture of her skin and the momentary void of her eyes. Her jet black hair was tangled and fell around her shoulders while she clutched the front of a cheap bathrobe together to keep it closed.

I pushed her inside, took Dulcie with me and closed the door. Greta had gone pretty far down the line. The room was bare as the law allowed. One closet showed only a few clothes and an empty gin bottle lay on the nightstand beside the bed with a broken glass on the floor.

She looked from me to Dulcie, then back to me again. "What do you want?"

"You, Greta," I said.

"What for? What the hell do you mean by

. . . ?" She stopped, took a longer look at me, then added, "Don't I know you?"

"Mike Hammer."

Then she knew me. "You bastard," she hissed.

"Ease off, kid. Don't blame your brother's fall on me. He was the one who wanted me to find you."

Greta took a step back, faltering a little. "Okay, you found me. Now get out of here." For some reason she avoided looking at my eyes.

"What's with this bit?" I asked her.

Her head came up hesitantly, her lips tight. "Leave me alone."

"Harry wants to see you."

She spun around, staring dully into the dirty glass of the window. "Like this?"

"I don't think he cares."

"Tell him for me that I'll see him when I'm ready."

"What happened, Greta?"

We exchanged glances in the reflection of the glass. "I didn't make it, that's all. I had big ideas and they didn't work out."

"So what do I tell Harry?"

"I'm working," she said. "I make a buck here and there. My time will come." There was a funny catch in her throat. When I didn't answer she spun around, her hands going to her hips. The robe came open as she stood there glaring at me and under the nightgown her body was outlined in lush perfection. "Just tell him to stay off my back until I'm ready, you hear me? And quit following me around. I'll do what I want to do my own way and I don't need any interference. He didn't do so good his way either, did he? All right, at least I'm on the outside doing what I can. Now lay off me and get out of here!"

"Greta . . . want to talk about Helen Poston?"

There was no physical reaction at all. "She's dead. She killed herself."

"Why?"

"How would I know? She'd been brooding over some man. If she was stupid enough to kill herself over one she deserved it."

"Maybe she didn't kill herself," I said.

A small shudder crossed her shoulders and her hands were clenched into fists. "When you're dead you're dead. What difference does it make any more?"

"Not to her. It could to somebody else. Feel like talking about it?"

She turned angrily and walked to the closet, tore the clothes from the hangers and threw them into a suitcase on the floor. "Damn it," she muttered, "I'll go someplace where nobody can find me." She looked back over her shoulder, eyes blazing. "Go on, get out of here!"

Dulcie said, "Can't we do something?"

"No use. This is what I came for. Come on, let's go."

On the street there were a pair of cabs parked off the corner. I put Dulcie in the first, told her to wait a second, then walked back to the other cab. I wrapped a five-spot around my card and handed it to the driver. He took it cautiously, his eyes wary. I said, "There may be a woman coming out of that hotel in a few minutes. If she takes a cab, you pick her up. Let me know where she goes and I'll make it worth your while."

He held the card under the dash light and when he looked up there was a big grin on his face. "Sure, Mike," he said. "Hot damn."

Dulcie McInnes lived in a condominium apartment that rose alongside the park with quiet splendor that only the very wealthy could afford. I knew some of the names of others who owned their premises there and I was surprised Dulcie could afford it. She saw the question in my face and said, "Don't be surprised, Mike. The Board of Directors of Proctor insisted on it. Something to do with image-making, and since they own the building, I am happy to comply with their wishes."

"Nice. I should have a job like that."

"At least you can share my luxury after taking me to that . . . that place tonight."

"It's pretty late."

"And it's coffee time . . . or are you a little old-fashioned?"

I let out a little laugh and followed her into the elevator. The air whooshed in the tunnel we were being sucked up in, the quiet sound of unseen machinery humming in some distant place. Little voices, I thought. They were saying something, but were too far away to be heard. It wasn't like the old days any more. I could think faster then. The little things didn't get by me. Like tonight at the Sandelor Hotel. Everything was fine. I could tell Harry that. I did what he wanted me to do. Greta was on her uppers, but well enough and I couldn't blame her for not wanting Harry to see her. She could have known the dead girls, but that wouldn't be unusual at all. Greta was alive. She wanted it the way it was. Then what was so damn peculiar?

I hadn't realized the elevator had stopped and I was staring past Dulcie, who stood in a small foyer, past the arch into a magnificent living room whose windows looked like living pictures of New York with its myriad of winking lights.

"Remember me?" she smiled. "We're here." She reached her hand out, took mine and led me inside. "Drink or coffee?"

"Coffee," I said. "You sure your friends won't object to me being here?"

"Friends?"

"Some of the company you travel in ranks pretty high."

Dulcie giggled again, a disturbing quality that made her seem schoolgirlish. "Some are just rank. Now sit down while I put the coffee on." She disappeared into the recesses of the house, but I could hear her making domestic sounds, unconsciously whistling snatches of a new show tune. I turned the record player on, slipped a few Wagnerian selections on the spindle and turned the volume down so the challenging themes were reduced to mere suggestions of their intent.

She came back with the coffee and set it on the marble-topped table in front of the sofa and sat down beside me. "You're awfully pensive. Do I affect you that way?"

I took the coffee from her and studied her face. Even this close, maturity had only softened her beauty to classic form. Her breasts swelled beneath the sweater, melted into hips poised in an arrogant twist, with her legs crossed, one in gentle motion. "Not you," I grinned.

"Thinking about Greta Service, weren't you?"

"A little."

She stirred her coffee and tasted it. "Weren't you satisfied?"

"Not really. I wish I knew why."

Dulcie put her cup down and leaned back thoughtfully. "I know. Unfortunately, I've seen it happen before. Some of these girls never realize what a tough world this is. There are thousands of beautiful faces and gorgeous bodies. They aspire for greatness and when it doesn't happen to them they can't understand it. The road downhill is steeper than the one going up."

"It's not that. She's been kicked around before. I thought she was a more determined type."

"Frustration can be a pretty terrible thing," she said. "What can you do?"

"Nothing, I guess. I'll just lay it out the way it is. Her brother will have to be satisfied with it."

"And you'll never have another reason for disrupting my routine again," Dulcie smiled impishly.

"Maybe I'll think of one."

The light glinted from her eyes when she stared at me, the pupils dark little pools under long, curling lashes. Her tongue stole out, moistened her lips and very softly, very directly, she said, "Think of one now," then reached up and turned off the light above us.

She was a gentle, lovely flower that budded slowly, then erupted into a wild blossom of incredible delight. Her hands were tight on my wrists, directing their motion, controlling pressures to her own satisfaction, then, knowing I understood, began a searching of their own. Her mouth was a delectable pillow of warmth that moaned with pleasure when I kissed her, her entire body a writhing masterpiece of sensuality.

When the gray light of the false dawn touched the city outside, I left and took a cab to the Carter-Layland Hotel. I got the key to my room, went in quietly and kicked off my shoes. The door to the adjoining bedroom was closed, so I lay down on the bed and stared at the ceiling, my hands under my head.

All I could think of . . . was it over or just beginning?

chapter seven

I never remembered having fallen asleep. I awoke with the fading light of day suffusing the room and the mice feet of rain on the window beside the bed. My watch said ten minutes to four and I swore under my breath for letting time get away from me.

When I rolled out of the sack a note fell off my chest. *Blue Ribbon at six, stinker,* it read and was signed with Velda's elaborate V. A quick shower straightened me out, I shaved the stubble off my face and pawed through the suitcase of clothes she had brought for me and got dressed. Automatically, I checked the action on the .45, slipped it into the holster and pulled my coat on.

Last night had been a rough one. I grinned, reached for the phone and dialed Dulcie's office number. The one who answered was Miss Tabor, the old maid I had ruffled so badly the first time around. When I asked for Dulcie she said Miss McInnes had left for Washington on the ten o'clock plane and would be out of town for several days. She asked who was calling and when I told her I could hear her quick gasp and she stammered that she would tell Miss McInnes that I had called.

I hung up the phone and started to get up when it rang. I picked it up again and said, "Yes?"

"This Mike Hammer?"

"You got him."

"Ray Tucker, Mike. I'm the cab driver you told to follow that girl last night."

I had damn near forgotten about that. "Sure, Ray. Where'd she go?"

"Well, it's hard to say. She came out and flagged me down and I took her to that five-story public parking lot on Eighth and Forty-sixth. She hopped out and went inside. The gate was closed on one side so I cruised around the other and waited a few minutes, then a car came out I think was her. I was going to follow her a ways, but a passenger boarded me and I was laying back too far to really tail her. She drove down to Seventh, then turned right again on the block where there's a southbound entrance to the West Side Highway. That's the best I could do."

"Get the make of the car?"

"A light blue Chevy sedan. A new one. Couldn't spot the plates," he said. Then suddenly he added, "Oh, yeah, there was a dent in the right rear fender. Just a little one."

"Okay, Ray, thanks. Let me know where to reach you and I'll send you a check."

"Forget it, Mike. Them things are kind of fun." He hung up and I put the phone back.

There it was again. Something that didn't belong there. You don't own a new car while you're bedding down in the squalid quarters of the Sandelor Hotel. But Ray Tucker wasn't sure, either and if the driver in the car wasn't Greta Service, she could have used the parking lot as a cute gimmick to check on anyone following her. I knew the place, and while one side was open to traffic, the gate on the other merely admitted a person and not a car. If she thought I might have been on her tail it would have been a perfect spot to dump me.

I grabbed my hat and raincoat, went downstairs, checked for messages, then went out and waited five minutes before a cab pulled over for me. I gave him the address of the Sandelor Hotel and sat back. I don't usually get mistaken for a tourist, but the cabbie took a chance on it. He caught my eyes in the rear-view mirror and said, "If anybody steered you to the broads in that place, buddy, drop it."

"No good?" I asked absently.

"Crap. You'd do better with a pick-up from one of the joints. That's real gook stuff there."

The tautness started across my mouth. "Oh?"

"Sure, foreign seamen, weirdie boys, all that. Maybe half a dozen broads work outa that place and I wouldn't pay five cents to throw a rock at it."

"I'm not after a dame. There may be a friend of mine there."

He shook his head sympathetically. "Tough," he muttered. "That's a real bughouse."

There was a new man on the desk this time, a

tall sallow-faced guy in a worn blue serge suit with rodent eyes that seemed to take everything in at once without moving at all. When I passed the desk he said, "Say . . ." in a whispery voice and I turned, walked back again and stood there for a good ten seconds without taking my eyes off him.

He tried to bluster it out, but it was the kind of situation he didn't like. "Can I . . . help you?"

"Yeah. You can stay right there and keep your mouth shut. Is that plain enough?"

Those narrow little eyes half shut and the rodent look turned snakelike. He passed it off with a shrug and went back to his bookkeeping. I went up the stairs and down the corridor to the room I had been in last night.

This time the light was already on, and inside a man's hoarse voice was spitting obscenities at a girl. She came back at him with some vile language, then there was the fleshy sound of a hand cracking across a jaw and I shoved the door open.

She sprawled on the floor against the wall, momentarily stunned, one hand pressed against her cheek, a dirty blonde life had prematurely aged. The guy was a big one, heavy under the sport coat and slacks, his face showing the signs of a losing ring career. His nose was flattened and twisted, one ear lumpy and a scar dragged down one corner of his mouth.

He looked at me with a sneer and said, "You got the wrong room, buster."

"I got the right one."

Surprise turned the sneer into a half-smile of anticipation. "Out, out. Like maybe you don't know any better?"

I just stood there. He let two seconds go by, then dropped into a familiar crouch and came at me. He started to feint with his left to cross one over to my jaw, only I never let him get that far. I put a straight jab in his mouth that jarred him back, then hooked him in the gut and again under the chin before he realized what had happened. His legs went rubbery and he went into a sagging dance of defeat. I made sure of it with another right that almost snapped his head off and he crashed against the lone dresser and knocked the lamp off it.

The girl was looking up at me with outright fear, wide awake now. "What . . . did you do . . . that for?"

"Be happy, kid. He belted you, didn't he?"

She started to struggle to her feet. I yanked her up, led her to the bed and let her sit down. "We . . . hell, he's my . . . we work together." Anger flooded her face and she spoke through clenched teeth. "You damn fool, now he'll beat the hell out of me. You crazy or something? What did you make trouble for? Why don't you go . . . ?"

I held out my wallet so she could see the glint of metal inside. Like I figured, she wasn't the kind who wanted to question a badge so far as even take a good look at it. Tiny white lines etched the corners of her mouth and she threw a nervous glance at the guy on the floor. "Let's start with names," I said.

There wasn't any anger in her voice any more. "Listen, mister . . ."

"Names, kid. Who are you?"

She looked down at her feet, her fingers twisting at the bedclothes. "Virginia Howell."

"Where's Greta Service?"

I saw her frown, then she looked up at me. "I don't know any Greta Service."

Too many times I had put up with lying broads and I could tell when they were spinning one off. *This one wasn't. Now it was all back to where it started again.*

"Let's start with last night, Virginia. Where were you?"

"I was . . . out on a trick." She dropped her eyes again.

"Go on."

"It . . . was a hotel on Forty-ninth. Some john from out of town, I guess. Probably from one of the ships. He . . . he wasn't nothing, but he gave me a hundred bucks and I spent the night with him."

"Where'd you pick him up?"

"I didn't." She pointed to the guy on the floor. "He arranged the date like most of the time. He don't like me doing my own business." A touch of irony came into her voice. "I suppose I got to split with you too. Well, get it off him. He got it all now. Never even let me keep my percentage because I gave him some lip."

140

"You let anybody use your room?"

"Who the hell wants to use this dump?"

"I didn't ask that."

"No," she said.

I stepped over the guy on the floor. He was breathing heavily through his nose and a trickle of blood was dribbling down his chin. I opened the door of the closet. The same rack of clothes and suitcase was there that I had seen last night.

Virginia said, "You'd better blow, mister. He hates cops."

"Who is he, kid?"

"Lorenzo Jones. He used to fight."

"He's not doing so good right now."

"Just the same, he's mean. Don't think he won't look for you."

I bent over and plucked Lorenzo Jones' wallet from his pocket. He had five hundred and thirty bucks in it, a driver's license issued to himself giving the hotel as his permanent address and two tickets to the fight at the Garden next week. "Where's his room?"

Virginia made a disgusted grimace. "Who knows? He's got six girls in his string. Whoever's empty that night is where he stays. He won't pay for anything. He says he lives here. That's a lot of bull. He used to before he took on the other girls."

"Let's get back to last night again."

She sighed, squeezed her eyes shut and named the hotel, the room and the man as simply "Bud." He was middle-aged, dark, had a trace of an accent and a scar on his chin. Lorenzo Jones had met her at their usual place at eleven o'clock, told her where to go and she went. The whole arrangement had been customary as far as she was concerned except that Jones had bragged about how he had taken the sucker for a bundle. Remorsefully, she added, "You know something, mister? Two years ago I was getting two hundred bucks a night every time."

"These streets go two ways, kid. You don't have to stay around."

"Cut it out. Where the hell is there to go?"

I threw Lorenzo's wallet on the bed and reached down to jerk him to his feet. The voice from the doorway said, "Just hold it like that."

A pair of them stood there, one blocking the doorway with his body, the other slapping a billy against his palm suggestively. They were gutter punks trained in countless street brawls and the kind of predators who were turning the city into a shambles. They were in their late twenties, dangerous as hell because they liked what they were doing and were completely equipped for it.

The first one sensed what I was going to do and moved like a cat. Before I could get the .45 in my hand he was on me, swung the billy in a flat arc and I got my arm up just in time to deflect it. The thing caught me high on the shoulder and my whole arm went numb. He started a back-hand swing when I chopped a short one up between his legs. He let out a breathless yell, but I hadn't caught him squarely enough and he was

142

back again, cursing through his teeth. The other one came in from the door, launched a round-house right into my ribs, knocking me back against the bed and sending Virginia to the floor. He saved my neck because he knocked me out of the way of the billy, but I didn't have time to think about it.

Maybe they thought I was going to use my hands. They should have known I had been through the mill too. I braced myself, kicked out and smashed the second guy's face to a pulp with my heels, rolled, got to my feet, stepped into the clear and let the one with the billy make another try for me. He came in grinning, tried to fake me out and brought his arm around. I went under it, caught his forearm, threw him into a lock and went against the elbow joint with such leverage that the bone splintered under my fingers and the guy jerked like a crazy puppet with the ago-nizing pain that tore through his body. For one second his mouth opened to scream, then he went limp in a faint and I let him drop to the floor. The other one was on his hands and knees, trying to get up. I kicked him in the face again and he flopped back like a big rag doll.

Virginia Howell was crouched in the corner, hands pressed to her mouth, eyes great staring orbs of fear. There wouldn't be any use trying to talk to her now. I picked up my hat and looked around.

Lorenzo Jones was gone.

I went downstairs and when the desk clerk saw

me coming, he turned pale. He didn't move when I grabbed his shirt front, didn't make a sound when I backhanded him across the mouth three times. He was caught short and was paying for it, hoping the others would be as easy on him. While he watched, I picked up the phone, called Pat and told him what happened. Everything was turning screwy and we'd want a pickup on Greta Service no matter what the excuse would be, and one on Lorenzo Jones, which would be easy to make stick. He told me to stand by to give the details to the squad car that was on the way, but I didn't have any intention of doing that at all. Those boys knew how to get what they wanted and the ones upstairs would still be here when they arrived.

In fifteen minutes I was supposed to meet Velda. She was going to have to wait. I went back into the rain, walked two blocks north along the curb, trying to spot an empty cab, finally flagged one down and had him take me to the Proctor Building.

The attendant in the lobby had just come on duty and told me the staff had already left for the day, but he was the same one who had been there last night and remembered me being with Dulcie. I told him she had asked me to get something from Theodore Gates' office, that it was damn important and somebody's head would roll if her wishes weren't complied with. He was so eager to please that he called his assistant in to watch the lobby and took me upstairs himself.

When we reached Gates' office I went directly to his rotary card file and spun it around to the G's. What I wanted was those symbols he had inscribed there and to get them translated. I thought I had missed her name and tried again, then a third time to be sure.

Greta Service's card was missing.

The attendant was watching me closely. "Find what you needed, sir?"

I didn't answer him. Instead, I asked, "Who's the receptionist on this floor?"

He thought a moment, then: "A Miss Wald, I believe."

"I want her home phone."

"There's probably a directory in the desk there." He went to the top drawer, pulled out a slide and ran his finger down it. "Here you are." He read the number off to me. I picked up the phone and dialed it. After four rings a young voice answered and I said, "Miss Wald, I'm calling for Theodore Gates. Was he in the office today?"

"Why, yes, he was. He came in about ten, but canceled his appointments and left."

"Know where I can reach him?"

"Did you try his home?"

"Not yet."

"Then I don't know where he could be. You'll have to wait until tomorrow."

I told her thanks and hung up. I found his home number, dialed it, let it ring a dozen times before I was sure there was nobody there, then hung up and jotted down his address.

"Will that be all, sir?"

"Yeah," I said. "For now."

Gates had a combination studio apartment in a renovated brownstone in the Fifties. Two other photographers occupied the building and apparently the one on the bottom floor was working because the lights were on and the foyer door open. I went inside, up the stairs to the second floor and pushed the buzzer to Gates' apartment.

Nobody answered.

I tried six picks on the lock before getting one that worked, stepped inside and felt for the light, the .45 tight in my fist. I flipped it on, moved sideways and covered the room. The place was a maze of equipment, smelling of hypo and water-colored backdrops, but it was empty. I tried each of the rooms to make sure. Theodore Gates wasn't there. Two closets were still full of his clothes, his dresser drawers well filled and orderly, but there was no telling whether or not he had taken anything with him.

In the studio itself was a desk cluttered with photographic supply catalogues and opened mail, another of those rotary files centered on it. I thumbed through this one too, but there was no Greta Service in it either. Along one side was a row of metal filing cabinets and I pulled out the one under "S." A folder of proofs on Greta Service was there, all right, duplicates of the ones in the Proctor Building. I was about to shut the

146

drawer when I noticed that the contents had been alphabetically arranged from the P's to the T's. Out of curiosity I thumbed the first few back.

Then I saw the name *Helen Poston.*

Only four proofs were in the folder, but they were enough. Teddy Gates had posed her so that every inch of her lush form was visible through the sheer Grecian gown, the same one Greta had modeled in. She wasn't a Proctor Girl, but neither was Greta. It was too bad. They made the Proctor Girls look pretty sickly. I put the proofs back and tried the "D" file and came up with three on Maxine Delaney. The redhead wore a sarong, but the effect was the same. All woman, but no Proctor Girl. There was too much breast and thigh, too much inborn seductiveness rather than the lean emaciated look the fashion magazines demanded.

I closed the drawers and checked the rotary file again. Neither Helen Poston nor Maxine Delaney had an index card there. That I could expect. They were both dead. Taking their photos out of the files would come with a general cleanup. But Greta Service's *had* been there and wasn't any longer.

Any prints I might have left, I wiped off, then went downstairs, back to Broadway where I picked up a cab and headed for the Blue Ribbon.

Velda had almost given me up and was on her last cup of coffee. Angie was trying to keep her company at a table in the back, but they had run out of conversation just as I arrived. She had sparks in her eyes and if there had been something to throw I would have caught it, but she took one look at my face where the guys at the Sandelor had worked me over and the anger subsided into an expression of concern and she grabbed for my hand.

Angie brought me coffee and a sandwich and while I finished it I gave her the details. The little fine points I would liked to have elaborated on wouldn't come out. They were still ideas that wouldn't congeal into a solid and until they did they just lay there dormant, oozing through my mind, waiting to be recognized.

Velda had had a phone pickup service put on the office line and the only ones who had called were Hy and Pat. Pat had two possibles on persons who had been convicted on sex charges, later paroled and were presumed to be in the area. Both were parole violators and an intensive search was on for both. The men who jumped me were in custody, accusing the desk clerk of having hired them to lay me out. I was supposed to go in and press charges. There was a tracer out for Lorenzo Jones, but a guy like that could disappear anywhere in New York. Virginia Howell came up with the names and addresses of his other women, but he wasn't at any of those places.

Hy wanted to see me as soon as possible. Al Casey had come up with something he wanted corroborated and I was to meet him at ten at his office.

148

When Velda had given me the information she said, "What does it look like?"

"It smells. When it gets this damn complicated there's something else going on."

"I found the car Greta Service used. It was a rental job and she had it out twice. Both times it was registered to her and the mileage figures were nearly identical. The first time it was 118 miles, the second, 122." She reached in her pocketbook and brought out a map of the New York, Jersey and Long Island area.

"Figuring it as a round trip each way," she said, "I laid out a general sixty-mile radius from the city. Here it is." She shoved the map to me and sketched the circled area with her forefinger.

"That's a hell of a lot of square miles," I told her.

"We're only interested in the perimeter."

"If she went directly to her target, yeah."

"We'll have to assume some things. Anyway, she had Helen Poston with her and women don't usually get too devious when they're driving."

I traced the line of her circle, picking out the cities the line touched. Peculiarly, there weren't many that it intersected at all. According to the diagram, the extent of Greta's trip would have led her to some pretty remote spots.

There was one that it did come close to, though. It was on Long Island and the name was *Bradbury.* I took out my pen and drew a circle around the town. "We'll start here."

She looked across the table at me and nodded.

"The origin of that letter Greta had."

"When Harry mentioned it she cut him off. It may mean something."

"I know the section, Mike. When I was a kid it was a very exclusive place for the wealthy. It's come down a lot since the general population move to the suburbs, but there are still a lot of big people out that way."

"Who would Greta know there?" I asked her.

"A beautiful woman might know anybody. At least it's a lead. Supposing I check into a hotel out that way and see what I can do. I'll call you when I'm located."

"You watch it. You're a beautiful doll too."

"It's about time you noticed." She gave me a big grin. "And when I think of those lovely adjoining rooms going to waste . . ."

"I'm hurting too, kitten."

She looked at her left hand and the ring I had given her. "I can come closer to getting married than any girl in the world. Why did I have to pick you?"

"Because we're made for each other," I told her. "Now get moving."

I could tell when Pat was burning. He stared at me with those cold eyes of his as if I were a suspect and let me go through my story for the third time around before he said, "Just tell me why you didn't hold Greta Service."

"For what reason?"

"You could have called me."

"Sure, and if there was something backing up this mess and she's involved she would have clammed right up."

"That doesn't cut it with me, Mike."

"No? I'd like to see what a lawyer would do to you if you tried it. I played it my way and that's the way it is. Any word on Lorenzo Jones or Gates yet?"

"Not a damn thing. Jones is holed up somewhere and the best we got on Gates was a statement from the elevator operator in the Proctor Building that he left sometime after ten. He carried no luggage and seemed to be in a hurry. The cleaning woman who took care of his place said everything was still there as far as she knew, but she had the idea he kept a woman somewhere and a change of clothes at her apartment. We're still looking. Incidentally, the other desk clerk at the Sandelor Hotel handed us a blank. He knew the Howell dame but couldn't identify Greta. He's generally half in the bag and can't see too well anyway. We leaned on him a little but couldn't cut it at all."

"And Dulcie McInnes?"

"She was on live TV from Washington this afternoon M.C.-ing a fashion show for some big women's organization. She's a house guest of a woman who's the wife of one of our biggest lobbyists and couldn't give us a lead to Gates at all. She suggested that he might have gone off on an independent assignment. Our men didn't think so because the equipment he would have carried is still at his studio."

I leaned back in the chair with my hands folded behind my head. "Not much is being said in the papers about Mitch Temple."

"Which is the way we wanted it and they're cooperating."

On the wall the clock ticked the seconds away. Pat finally said "The M.E. had replies to his queries about the poison that was used on the Poston girl. It wasn't as exclusive as he thought it was. There are certain other derivatives from similar sources that have been used by the Orientals for centuries. It went out of fashion when the royalty class was deposed by the rabble, but available. Interpol reported its use several times during some big family vendettas in Turkey."

"I'm missing your point," I said.

Pat picked up a pencil and doodled on a pad on the desk. "There isn't any. I'm just throwing it up for grabs."

"Sorry, buddy."

"We hit a dead end on the whip that killed the Delaney kid."

"You still have one more to go. Find out who owns a rack."

Pat shot me an annoyed glance. "Mike . . . this could be an individual. A nut. He preys on one type. He uses gimmicks." He threw the pencil down and slapped the desk with an open hand. "Damn it, I haven't got the feeling that it is and neither do you."

I didn't say anything.

"Damn it, Mike . . ."

"Something's wrong. Too many things miss being on the line by a fraction. There are people involved who have no right being there at all. Kills like this generally touch only certain persons . . . they don't get spread out all over the map like this one." I stopped and let the chair ease forward. "No, I don't think it's an individual. It's too well coordinated. If it were an individual somebody would have seen something. If those kills were related there was nothing spontaneous about them."

"Get to it, Mike."

"Theodore Gates could be the key. He knew three of them. Photos of them were in his files. I saw Greta's name in his personal index and the next time it wasn't there at all. He had the time to destroy it. Greta could have called him after I left there to tell him I had located her. A little thought would put his finger on what happened. He took the card out and disappeared."

"Why?"

"And therein lies the rub," I quoted. "Why? Unless he and Greta had something going for them. Somebody obviously paid off Lorenzo Jones to use Virginia Howell's room that night. I'll take her word for it she didn't know what the scoop was."

"We'll get him."

"Sure, but what good will it do? He's a pimp, a punchy pimp. If there's a hot one here nobody's going to invite him in on the deal. That type is too likely to blow it to pieces. No, he was used somehow. I can see how a guy like Gates might have had contact with Jones. Gates had outside assignments that could have led to Jones or he just could have been one of the guy's clients. When you get a file on Gates that stuff will come out. We just can't wait around, that's all."

Pat got up and stalked to the window, snapping his fingers with impatience. "Mitch Temple puts it all in the same package," he said. "He spotted the same similarity and followed it up. He recognized somebody and died for it." He turned around and squinted at me. "Then there was that guy who tried for you. Nothing came of that either. We're dealing with a cast of nobodies."

"But they're there."

"Sure. And we're here. Three punks are in the can on an assault and battery charge. Great record. You know what the papers will be doing to this office if there's no action before long?"

I nodded. "Every reporter in the city is working overtime."

"The difference is, friend, that they don't have to be the goats."

"Pat," I said quietly.

"Yeah?"

"What's out at Bradbury?"

"Now what hole in your head did that come out of?"

"It came up along the line," I said.

Pat's smile was a tight thing that barely crinkled his mouth. There was no humor in it at all. Before he could push it I added, "Harry Service mentioned Greta having a letter from there once. He didn't see it."

Some of the frost left his face. "When was this?"

"Her last visit."

Pat went over it in his mind a moment and told me, "It's a resort area along the coast and a residential area for the wealthy further in. I haven't been there for five years."

"Nothing else?"

"You pushing an angle?" he demanded.

"Curious, that's all."

"She could have been there. The place is public beaches, a yacht harbor and motel area now. Some of the Fire Island crowd took it over and ran it down. It's getting a reputation of being an artists-and-models colony. The old permanent residents complained, but it didn't help any. I guess they thought it would ruin their image, especially after a couple of the embassies bought into the area there."

"What embassies?"

"Oh, the French have a place there . . . so do one of the Russian satellite countries. I think one of the Middle East outfits moved out there a couple of years ago too."

I laughed with surprise. "And I thought if it didn't happen in the city here you wouldn't know about it."

"The reason I know is because some of our best officers retired from the force to take up security jobs there at twice the pay."

"Not at the embassies?"

"No, they have their own security. The town has a jazz festival every year that brings in a mob of town wreckers. The public finally anted up for a bigger force before somebody caused an international incident. It's gotten worse every year. It's too damn bad Gerald Ute wouldn't be philanthropic in other fields."

"Ute?"

"Yeah, the one you met the other night."

"He's got a place out there?"

"Not him. He simply financed the jazz festivals. He turned his place into a communal recreation center for the bigwigs of the U.N. The city runs it, but on a pretty restricted basis. It was a grand gesture and got him a lot of publicity, but it got a white elephant off his hands too . . . along with a fat tax deduction."

He sat down, swinging idly in his chair, watching my face. "Velda's out there," I said.

"So are a hundred agents from Washington to make sure nothing happens to the housecats from the U.N. These days nobody wants to take a chance of having some politico scratched. Hell, the way diplomatic immunity goes these days we can't even give out parking tickets."

I didn't want Pat to see my face. He didn't know it, but he had just been the catalyst that jelled one of those thoughts that had been so damn elusive.

When I got up I tossed a note on Pat's desk.

"Can you see Harry gets this? It's a report that his sister is alive."

"Okay. You going to press charges against those three we're holding?"

"Right now."

"You're going to have a lot to talk about when you're in court on that kill."

chapter eight

Four of them were in the office when I got there. Al Casey and Hy were at the desk and two old-timers from the morgue file, passing them from one to another, identifying the subjects and making terse comments on their background.

I threw my coat and hat on a chair, took one of the containers of coffee from the sack and looked over Hy's shoulder. "What have you got?"

Hy nudged Al. "Tell him about it."

He fanned out a dozen pictures in front of him. "Mitch Temple pulled out a lot of folders, but his prints were only on the edges, from where he thumbed through them. However, on the photos in two of the folders his prints were all over them, so he had taken a lot of time going through them."

"These?"

"Yeah. Sixty-eight of them in the 'General Political' classification. We have everything from the mayor's speech to a union parley. We tried the cross indexes and can't see what ties in. Everybody in the foreground of the shots is identified and so far we have over three hundred names with repeats on about half, all of whom are fairly prominent citizens."

"How many did the paper use?"

"About a third. They're stamped on the back with the dates."

"There's a common denominator there though, isn't there?"

Hy nodded. "Sure. We nailed that right away. All were taken in New York within the last year. Try to make something out of that."

I picked some of the photos from the pile on the end and scanned through them. Some I remembered having seen in the paper, others were parts of the general coverage given the occasions by one or more photographers. There were faces I knew, some I had just heard about and too many that were totally unknown.

Every so often somebody would spot a possible connection and it would be checked out with another index, but every time they'd draw a blank. There didn't seem to be any possibility of a connection between their activities and Mitch Temple's death. Nevertheless, the pictures made repeated rounds among all of us.

I grinned when I saw Dulcie McInnes at a charity function and another of her at a ball in a Park Avenue hotel dancing with an elderly foreign ambassador in a medal-decorated sash. Then I stopped looking at faces and concentrated on the names typed and pasted to the back of the sheets.

The only one whose name had come up before was Belar Ris. He was greeting a diplomatic representative from one of the iron curtain countries who was getting off an airplane and Belar Ris had the funny expression of a man who didn't particularly care about being photographed. He seemed to be tall and blocky, suggestive of physical power even tailor-made clothes couldn't conceal. His face didn't show any trace of national origin except that he was swarthy and his eyes had a shrewd cast to them. His out-stretched arm was bared to the cuff of his coat, his wrist and forearm thick. Belar Ris was a short-sleeved-shirt man, the kind who wanted no obstacles in the way of a power move.

Al saw me concentrating on the photo and asked, "Got something?"

I tossed the picture down. "Mitch had some column items on this one."

He looked at it carefully. "Who didn't? Belar Ris. He's a U.N. representative. There's another picture of him in tonight's paper raising hell at an Assembly meeting."

"Anything special on him?"

"No, but he's publicity-shy. There are a dozen like him at the U.N. now . . . the grabbers. He'll play both ends against the middle to keep things going back home. Anything to protect his interests. It's too bad the idiots appoint people like that to represent them."

"They have to." Al separated some of the shots in front of him and picked one out. "Here's another of Ris. It was right after that Middle East blow-up. The guy he's talking to was ousted the next week and killed in a coup."

160

One other person was in the picture, but the lighting didn't make his features too distinguishable. "Who's this?"

Al took the picture from me, scanned it and shook his head. "Beats me. Probably in the background. He's not mentioned on the back."

"He looks familiar," I said.

"Could be. That's right outside the U.N. complex and he could be part of a diplomatic corps. It doesn't look like he's standing with Ris."

He was right. The guy wasn't with Ris or the other one, but it didn't look as if he were going anywhere either. He seemed to be in an attitude of waiting, but even then, with a stop-action shot, you couldn't tell. There was something vaguely familiar about him, a face you see once and couldn't forget because of the circumstances. I ran it through my mind quickly, trying to focus on possible areas of contact, but couldn't make a connection and put the picture back on the pile.

I spent another twenty minutes with them, then got up and wandered down the corridor to the morgue where old Biff was reading his paper. He waved and I said, "Mind if I take a look in your files?"

"Be my guest."

I went down the rows until I came to the "R's" and pulled out the drawer. There was a file on Belar Ris, with three indistinct photos that hadn't been used. There was the shadow of his hat, a hand apparently carelessly held in front of

161

his face and a blur of motion that didn't quite make him recognizable. The ones he was with were identified, but I didn't make any of them. All of them seemed to have some prominence, to judge by their clothes, the attaché cases they carried or the general background. I closed the files and walked back to the desk.

Hy was standing there looking at me.

"Okay, Mike," he said, "you pulled something out."

"Belar Ris," I told him. "There's nothing in the files."

"Why him?"

"Nothing special. He was the only one I recognized that Mitch wrote about."

"Can it, Mike. There *is* something special. What?"

"The guy doesn't seem to like having his picture taken."

"A lot of them are that way."

"Attached to a diplomatic staff? They're all publicity hounds."

"What do you know about Ris, Mike?"

"Only what Mitch wrote."

"Maybe I can tell you a little more. He's got a hush-hush background. Black-market activities, arms dealing, tricky business dealings, but I know a lot of others on top of the political situation that were just as bad. Right now he's being treated mighty carefully because guys like that can sway the balance of power in the U.N. Now look . . . there's something else about Ris, so don't you tell me . . ."

"There isn't anything, buddy. I was swinging wild."

Biff shoved the paper across the desk before Hy could answer me and said, "This the one you're talking about?"

It was Belar Ris on the front page, all right. He was talking to two of our people and a French representative during a break in the session and his face was hard and one finger pointed aggressively at our man who looked pretty damn disgusted. The caption said it was a continuation of the argument over having admitted the government represented by Naku Em Abor, who had just proposed some resolution inimical to the western powers.

Hy said, "Does that look like a guy who doesn't want his picture taken?"

I had to admit that it didn't.

Biff grinned and said, "Don't fool yourself, Hy. Charlie Forbes took that shot and he doesn't work with a Graflex. Ten to one it was a gimmick camera hidden under his shirt."

I tapped Hy on the shoulder. "See what I mean?"

He handed the paper back. "Okay, Mike. I'll buy a little piece of it. We'll poke around. Now how about the rest of it?"

"The boys on the police beat have big ears."

"When it concerns you, yeah."

I gave him the story on finding Greta Service without mentioning all the details, simply that

Dulcie McInnes had suggested checking Teddy Gates' files and I had come up with another address. He knew he wasn't getting the whole picture, but figured I was protecting a client's interest and since the job was done as far as Harry was concerned, it ended there.

When I left the building it was pretty late, but for what I wanted to do, the night was just starting.

The stable of girls Lorenzo Jones ran was a tired string operating out of run-down hotels and shoddy apartments. They all had minor arrest records, and after each one, simply changed the locality of their activities, picked up a new name and went back into the business. Like most of the girls who were on the tail end of the prostitution racket, they had no choice. Jones ran things with an iron fist and they didn't dispute his decisions. The operation was pretty well confined to the section catering to the waterfront trade, the quickies and drunks who patronized the dives where he made the contacts for his broads.

None of the first three I found had seen him and they seemed to be wandering around in a vacuum, not knowing whether to hit the streets or wait for Jones to arrange their appointments. Two of them had turned repeat tricks for old customers out of habit and one had solicited a couple of customers on her own because she was broke.

For some reason they were anxious to see Jones show up again, probably because on their own they'd get sluffed off if they tried to hustle, while Jones got the money in advance and the customer took what he was offered whether he liked it or not.

Talking wasn't part of their makeup. They had taken too many lumps from Jones and their customers over the years and there was no way to lean on them.

But the fourth one wasn't like that. Her name was Roberta Slade and she was the last one Jones had added to his firm. I found her in a place they called Billy's Cave sipping a martini and studying herself in the mirror over the back bar.

When I sat down her eyes caught mine in the glass and she said with a voice the gin had thickened just a little bit, "Move to the rear of the bus, mister."

She turned insolently and I could see that one time she had been a pretty girl. The makeup was heavy, her eyes tired, but there was still some sparkle in her hair and a little bit of determination in the set of her mouth. "Do I know you?"

I waved for a beer and pushed some money across the bar. "Nope."

"Well, I'm taking the day off." She turned back and twirled the glass in her hand.

"Good for you," I said.

I finished half the beer and put the glass down. "Shove off," she said softly.

I took twenty bucks out and laid it down between us. "Will that buy some conversation?"

A little grin split her lips and she glanced at me, her eyebrows raised. "You don't look like one of those nuts, mister. I've given a hundred different versions of my life history embellished with lurid details to guys who get their kicks that way and I can spot them a city block away."

"I'm not paying for that kind of talk."

Quickening interest showed in her face. "You a cop? Damn, you look like one, but you can't tell what a cop looks like any more. The vice squad runs college boys who look like babies; dames you take for schoolteachers turn out to be police-women. It's rough."

"I'm a private cop, if you want to know."

"Oh boy," she laughed. "Big deal. Whose poor husband is going to get handed divorce papers for grabbing some outside stuff?" She laughed again and shook her head. "I don't know names, I'm lousy at remembering faces and all your twenty bucks could buy you would be a lot of crap, so beat it."

"I want Lorenzo Jones."

The glass stopped twirling in her fingers. She studied it a moment, drained it and set it on the bar. "Why?" she asked without looking at me.

"I want to give him a friendly punch in the mouth."

"Somebody already did."

"Yeah, I know." I laid my hand palm down on the bar so she could see the cuts across my knuckles. "I want to do it again," I said.

166

Very slowly, her face turned so she was smiling up at me and her eyes had the look of a puppy that had found a friend and was trying his best not to run away. "So I have a champion."

"Not quite."

"But you laid him out, didn't you? Word gets around fast. You were the one who raised all that hell in Virginia's room, weren't you?"

"I was on a job."

Her grin turned into a chuckle and she motioned with a finger for the bartender to fill her glass again. "I wish I could have seen it. That dirty bastard took me apart enough times. He hated my guts, you know that? And do you know why?"

"No."

"I used to work a hatcheck concession in a joint he hung out in. I wasn't like this then. He tried his best to make me and I brushed him off. He was a pig. You know how he gets his kicks? He . . . well, hell, that's another story."

Her drink came and I paid for it. For a few seconds she stirred the olive around with the toothpick absently, then tasted it, her eyes on herself in the back bar mirror. "I almost had it made. I was doing some high-class hustling, then I got a guy who liked me. Nice rich kid. Good education." She made a sour grimace and said, "Then Jones queered the deal. He got some pictures of me on a date and showed them to the kid. That was the end of that. I went to pieces, but he picked them up fast. He had me worked over a couple of times, picked up by the cops so I had a record, then he moved in and took over when I didn't have any place to go." Roberta took a long pull of the martini and added sadly, "I guess this is what I was cut out for anyway."

"Where's Jones now?"

"I hope the bastard's dead."

"He isn't."

She ran the fingers of one hand through her hair, then lightly down the side of her cheek. "The cops are looking for him too."

"I know."

"Why?"

"There are a couple of dead girls he might know something about."

"Not Lorenzo Jones. They can't make any money for him dead. He'd keep them alive."

I said, "He's just a lead. I want him, Roberta."

"What will you do to him if you find him?"

"Probably kick the crap out of him."

"Promise?"

I grinned at her. She wasn't kidding at all. "Promise," I said.

"Can I watch?"

"My pleasure."

She picked the drink up, looked at it a moment, then put it down unfinished. The twenty was still there, but she didn't touch it. "My treat," she told me.

The rain had slicked the pavement and was coming down in a fine drizzle, throwing a misty halo around the street lights. I wanted to call a cab, but Roberta said no and we walked two blocks without talking. Finally I said, "Where to?"

"My place." She didn't look at me.

"Lorenzo there?"

"No, but I am." She didn't say anything after that, crossing the avenues in silence, then down another two blocks until we came to the doorway between a pair of stores and she took my arm and nodded. "Here."

She put a key in the lock and pushed the door open, stepped in and let me follow her. I went up the stairs behind her, waited at the first landing while she opened up again and switched the light on. I had been in a lot of cribs before and they were usually dingy affairs, but she had taken a lot of trouble with this one. It was a three-room apartment, clean, furnished simply, but in good taste.

Roberta saw me take it in with a single sweep of my eyes and caught my initial reaction. "My early upbringing." She walked to the closet, reached deep into the shelf and came out with a cheap pad stuffed with papers and held together with a rubber band. She handed it to me and said, "He dropped it one night. It's a tally sheet on us, but you'll find receipts in there from a few places. We knew he had a place he stayed when he wasn't in with one of us, but nobody knew where. That is, until I found this one night. You'll find him there, but let me go find me first."

I looked at her, wondering what the hell she was talking about, and when she left, sat down and opened the pad. The kids had made plenty for Lorenzo Jones, all right, but I wasn't interested in his take. What I saw were paid bills from three different small hotels, each covering a period for about three months, and the last was dated only a month ago and if the pattern fit, he'd be there now. Only he wasn't listed as Lorenzo Jones. His name on the bill head was an imaginative J. Lorenzo, room 614 of the Midway Hotel.

Roberta Slade came back then. She wasn't the same one who had left and I saw what she meant about finding herself. She smelled of the shower and some subtle perfume; the makeup was gone and the outfit she wore was almost sedate. She pulled on a maroon raincoat, stuffed her hair under a silly little hat and smiled gently. "There are times," she said, "when I hate myself and want to go back to what I think I could have been."

"I like you better this way."

She knew I meant it. There was an ironic tone in her voice. "It isn't very profitable."

"You could give it a try, kid."

"That depends on you. And Lorenzo Jones. He's got a long memory."

"Maybe we can shorten it up a little."

The Midway Hotel rented rooms by the hour or the day, and if you paid in advance no luggage was required. The going rate for accommodations was steeper than the place deserved because the management got its cut for providing its service of keeping its mouth shut and overlooking the preponderance of Smiths in the register.

I signed in as Mr. and Mrs. Thompson from Toledo, Ohio, passed the money over and took the key marked 410. The clerk didn't even bother to look at my signature or thank me for letting him keep the change of my bill.

There was no bellhop, but this place had an early-model self-service elevator that took us to the fourth floor where we got out. We walked to the room and when I opened the door she gave me an odd look, a wry little smile, shrugged and walked in.

I grinned at her, but there wasn't any humor there. "No tricks, kid. I can't go busting in his door up there and he damn well won't open it for me."

"Nothing would surprise me any more. I'm sorry."

I went to the window, forced it up and looked out at the back of the building. Like most, it had an iron fire escape with landings that covered the windows of several rooms at each floor. I shucked my raincoat and threw it to Roberta. "Give me fifteen minutes to get up there, then come pay a visit."

"You won't start without me, will you?"

"No . . . I'll wait."

Outside, thunder rumbled across the sky and for a second there was a dull glow over the city. I stepped out to the iron slats and closed the window behind me. The rain waited for that second and came at me like a basket of spitting cats, daring me to go any further.

I swung my legs over the railing and got my feet set, hanging on to the metal bar behind me. The rain pelted my face and I couldn't be sure of the distance to the other fire escape frame. Then the sky lit up with that dull gray incandescence and I could see it, and while the image was still there, jumped, my fingers clawing for the iron rail.

My hands made it, but my feet slipped, smashing me into the uprights. I hung on, pulled myself up until I found a toehold, then climbed over and stood there to get my breath and see if anybody had heard the racket. There wasn't any need to worry; the rain kept the windows closed and the thunder drowned out any noise I thought I made. Two flights up where room 614 was, the window was outlined in yellow behind the drawn shade.

I took the .45 out of the sling, cocked it and started up the stairs.

The window was open about four inches from the bottom with the shade pulled below the level of the sill. Inside a radio was playing some tinny music and the smell of cigar smoke seeped out the opening. There was a cough, the creak of bedsprings and somebody twisted the dial of the radio savagely until another station was on. I tried the window. The damn thing was stuck fast.

Behind my back the wind came at me, driving the rain through my clothes, making the shade flop against the sill. I edged to one side, reached out with my fingers, got the shade, pulled it down on the roller and let it go. The thing snapped up under the tension of the spring and flapped wildly around its axis and the guy on the bed jumped up with a curse, startled, a snub-nosed gun in his hand. He took a look at the shade, let out another curse, stuck the gun in his waistband and came to the window, reaching up to pull down the blind.

And saw me standing there with the .45 aimed at his middle through the glass.

"Open it," I said.

For a moment I thought he was going to try it, but the odds were just too big and he knew it. His face was a pasty white, his hands shook going to the window, and when he forced it up he stood there with the sweat running down his forehead into a crease in his flattened nose and he couldn't get a sound out of his throat.

I stepped inside, yanked the gun out of his pants and smashed him across the jaw with it. His head snapped back and he stumbled against the bed just as a knock came on the door. I walked over, opened it and let Roberta in. She gave me a hurt look and said, "You promised."

"It was just a teaser, kid," I told her. "The

main course comes up later."

Lorenzo Jones got his voice back. "Mister . . . look, I didn't do nothing. . . . I . . ."

"Shut up." I locked the door behind me, went over and pulled down the window, closed the shade and, very deliberately, turned the volume of the radio up.

Lorenzo Jones got the message loud and clear. His eyes in their heavy pads of flesh grew a little wild. They didn't want to look at mine. They tried to appeal to Roberta, then he saw who she was. "Look mister . . . if she paid you to do this, I'll pay you more. That bitch . . ."

"She didn't pay me, Lorenzo."

"Then why . . . ?"

"Shut up and listen to me, Lorenzo. Listen real good because I'm only going to say it once. I'm going to ask you questions and if you don't answer them right you're going to catch a slug someplace." I motioned to Roberta. "Get me a pillow."

She pulled one from the bed and tossed it to me. I wrapped it around the rod in my fist and walked over to Jones. He tried to swallow and couldn't. I said, "Who paid you to use Virginia Howell's room?"

"The . . . the girl. She . . ."

"Not the girl."

His nod was desperate. "It was, I'm telling you. She gimme the dough. . . ." I leveled the .45 at his kneecap. "Cripes, don't shoot me, will ya! I'm telling ya, the girl gimme the money. Ali said

174

she'd pay me. . . . It wasn't the first time. He wanted a room somewhere for himself or his friends, I'd clear Virginia out and let 'im use it. Always whoever used the room would pay me. He . . .

"Roberta?" I asked.

"He's pulled that plenty of times, usually with Virginia. A lot of those bums don't want to sign a register. A couple of times he stuck somebody up there who was hot."

I looked back to Jones again. "How long was Greta supposed to stay there, Lorenzo?"

His shrug was more like a big shudder. "I . . . dunno. Ali never told me. She got out on her own, then that stupid Virginia came back when I told her to stay away until I saw her. That's why I smacked her. She was givin' me a hard time. She didn't like nobody using her place. That other one messed up her clothes, threw them in a suitcase, knocked them down. . . ."

"That other one was putting on an act for me, Lorenzo. She wanted me to think she lived there." I stopped a second, watched him and said, "Was she there before?"

"How do I know? I don't ask Ali no questions. Maybe she was. I ain't gonna complain when . . ."

I cut him off. "Who's Ali?"

"Hell, that's all I know. Just Ali. He's a guy."

"You're getting close to hopping, Jones." I grinned at him and my mouth was a tight line across my teeth. I could feel my fingers starting to squeeze the gun.

Lorenzo Jones knew it too. His breath sucked in so hard he almost choked and he tried to double up in a ball. "Who's Ali?" I repeated.

His tongue ran over dry lips. "He's . . . on a ship. Some kind . . . of a steward."

"More."

"He brings things in. You know, he . . ."

"What does he smuggle, Jones?"

He couldn't keep his hands still and the sweat was dripping off his nose. "I . . . I think it's H. He don't tell me. His customers are . . . special. He ain't . . . in the rackets. He does it special."

"That puts him in the money class," I said.

Lorenzo jerked his head in a nod.

"How would he contact a slob like you?"

"I . . . got him some broads one time. He like to . . . well, he wasn't right. He did some crazy things to 'em, but he paid good."

"What things?"

Lorenzo Jones was almost babbling, but he said, "Cigarettes. He burned 'em, things like that. He'd . . . bite them. Once he . . ."

Roberta came up and stood beside me, looking at Jones with loathing. "I knew two of those kids. They never talked about it, but I saw the scars. One wound up in the mental ward at Bellevue and the other stepped in front of a subway train when she was dead drunk."

"Describe them, Jones."

His mind didn't want to work. He couldn't keep his eyes off the pillow that covered the gun in my hand. I grinned again and it was too much for him. His mouth began to contort into words. "He . . . he's kind of not too big like. He talks funny. I tried to get something on him so I could maybe score with him but he's careful. I seen him in the Village sometimes. Him and a silly hat. He goes with them oddballs down there for kicks. Look, I don't know him. He's just some gook."

I got that feeling again, a surging of little streams running together to churn into a more powerful feeder that would eventually build to a raging torrent. How many people had called other people a gook? It was old army slang for any native help, the baggy-pants bunch that toted your barracks bags and did your washing. The kind who'd beg with one hand and kill with the other, to whom petty theft was a pastime, robbery a way of life and to be caught was kismet and your head on a pole outside the city.

"Okay, Lorenzo, now one more for the big go and don't muff it. You said you tried to get something so you could score on him. That means you tailed him. You know he comes off a ship." I paused, then said, "Which ship?" and held the gun on his gut.

He didn't hesitate at all. "The *Pinella*."

I nodded. "Why you holing up, Lorenzo?"

No words came out. His eyes seemed sunk in the back of his head.

I said, "Maybe you did find out something. Maybe you found out this man would kill you the first time you ever messed anything on him."

Jones got his voice back at last. "Okay, so I seen those broads. I know guys like him. He even told me. He . . ." His voice lost itself in the fear that was so alive it drenched him with sweat.

"Now, Roberta?" I asked.

"Now," she said.

I took my time with him and any little sounds he was able to make were drowned in the noise of the radio. He came apart in small splashes of blood and livid bruises he was going to wear a long, long time. I talked to him quietly while I did it and before his eyes were closed all the way I made him look at Roberta and see what he had done to her and when he couldn't see any more, made him remember what he had done to the others. I made sure he knew that this could only be the start of things for him because a lot of people were going to know who he was and what he did and wherever he went somebody else would be waiting for him and Lorenzo Jones knew I wasn't lying, not even a little bit.

When it was over I took his wallet, emptied out the three grand it held and handed it to Roberta. She could split it up with the others and they could get the hell away from the mess they were in if they had the guts to. At least I knew she would.

I stuck the snub-nose gun in my pocket, put the .45 back and went downstairs with Roberta. I tossed the room key on the desk and the clerk put it back on the hook without looking at me. The rain had settled into a steady downpour and

I called a cab and put her in it.

She looked out the window, took my hand and said, "Thanks."

I winked at her.

"I don't even know your name," she said.

"It doesn't matter."

"No, it really doesn't, does it? But I won't forget you, big feller."

chapter nine

It wasn't too difficult to get a rundown on the *Pinella*. She was a freighter under Panamanian registry that accommodated ten passengers in addition to cargo. She had been in port eleven days taking on a load of industrial machinery destined for Lisbon and would be here another five days before sailing. The crew was of mixed foreign extraction under a Spanish captain and at the moment, most of them were ashore.

But it was almost impossible to get anything on the steward. His name was Ali Duval. He attended the passengers, generally engineers who traveled with the equipment, the crew and kept to himself on the ship. In port he left at the first possible moment and didn't return until just before sailing time. Both the Treasury men and the customs officials gave the ship and crew a clean bill of health. No contraband had ever been found on board, none of the crew had ever been apprehended trying to take anything illicit ashore and no complaint had ever been lodged against the vessel or its personnel.

During the lunch hour I circulated among some of the dock workers trying to pick up any information, but no one had anything to offer. A check through a friend of mine got me the story that the *Pinella* was owned by several corporations, but it would take months to unravel the front organizations and the real owners who buried themselves in a maze of paperwork to beat taxes.

I grabbed a bite to eat in a little restaurant, watching the dark creep up on the waterfront. The rain had stopped earlier, but it still was up there, threatening. The night lights came on along the wharves making the ships in their berths seem unreal and whoever walked between the lights and the hulls would throw a monstrous shadow along the steel sides momentarily, then dissolve into the dark further on.

I was going to grab a cab and head back uptown when I saw the night watchman come on duty across the street and decided to make another stab at it. In five minutes I found out he was a retired cop from the New York force who had been at this job ten years and glad to have somebody to talk to. The nights were long and lonely and conversation was the only thing left he had to enjoy.

And he knew Ali Duval. At least he knew who he was. On the ship he wore a uniform, but when he hit the beach he was wearing expensive clothes, which was pretty fancy for a low-paid steward, but he accounted for it by saying how guys like that saved their money and blew it in one big bust the minute they hit the shore. He used to wonder what it was he carried in the paper bag when he left the ship, then on two different occasions he had seen him drive up in a new black limousine wearing "one of them native hats like the Shriners wear."

I said, "A fez?"

"Yeah, that's it. With a tassel. He got out of the car, put it in the bag and went on board with his suitcase. Some of these foreigners are nuts."

"Who was in the car?"

"Got me. They were friends though. They sat and talked a few minutes, before he got out. I couldn't see the car. Sure was a dandy. Probably was a relative. Plenty of these guys got people over here, only usually they ain't so well off."

"Ever been on the ship?"

"Few times," he said. "The chow's pretty good."

"They get any visitors up there?"

"Not when I'm on. Hell, who wants to see a freighter? This one's better'n most, but she's still a freighter."

"Listen," I said, "how can I recognize this Duval?"

"Well, if he ain't got his hat on, you might say he's medium, kinda foreign-looking and has an accent. If you can read faces, I'd say this one could get mean if he wanted to, or maybe that's just the way some foreigners look. It's just that he's got . . . well, there's something."

"I know what you mean. Got any idea how I can find him?"

"Not a one. Couple of times the mate tried to dig him up, but that bird didn't show. He goes someplace and gets himself lost. Dames, probably. All them sailors think of is dames. The last time the mate chewed him out and wanted to know where the hell he was and Duval just looked at him like he wasn't even there and went up on deck. Guess he figures his shore time's his own. I know he don't go with none of the others. That bunch hardly ever gets more than six blocks away from here anyway. They're back and forth for their clothes, picking up money they left stashed away so they wouldn't get rolled for the whole wad the first night out and picking up chow on board when they go broke. This Duval, he just leaves and comes back as sharp as when he left. Sharper even. He's always got new clothes on."

I spent five more minutes with the old guy before I left but there wasn't any more he had to offer, so I thanked him and crossed the street to a bar and went in the back to a pay phone. I finally reached Pat at his apartment, told him I was coming up and to put the coffee on.

We sat there at the kitchen table of his bachelor digs and he listened while I gave him the bit at the Midway Hotel and the follow-up at the *Pinella*. When I got done he glared at me across the table and tossed his spoon halfway across the room in disgust. "Damn, when are you going to learn, Mike?"

"Jones wouldn't have told you any more."

"You know we have ways to handle guys like that."

"Balls. Those girls wouldn't file a complaint anyway."

"They don't have to. You think we couldn't get a witness to go against him?"

"So some judge would throw thirty days at him and let him go back into the business? Come on, Pat, you're smarter than that. He won't be operating in this town any more."

"Neither will you if the D.A, hears about it."

"Who's to tell?" I grinned. "Anyway, how about checking with Interpol to see if they have anything on Ali Duval."

"And then what?"

I finished my coffee and slid my chair back from the table. "Let's put the pieces together, Pat. You have three dead women who might have had some mutual relationship. I had one live one who's tied into the picture. We have a guy named Theodore Gates who knew at least three of them. I go looking for Greta Service and the lead took me to the Proctor Group. Dulcie said I caused a lot of talk up there. . . . It was right after the big spread they had on me in the papers, so supposing this Gates gets the word?"

Pat nodded agreement and rubbed his eyes

"Okay," I said, "so he remembered the file he had on Greta listing her with the Howell dame. Who knows what kind of photography he was doing? Half the pornography made is done in those joints. He got up to his office but the damage had already been done. He lifted the card out of the rotary file too late. Greta didn't want to be found, Gates didn't want her found, and when I did, Greta cut out. She could have contacted Gates and he took off when he saw things coming apart."

"I can punch holes in that," Pat said.

"But at least it's a place to start. And it gets us back to Mitch Temple. He was interested in the Delaney and Poston deaths too. He recognized somebody and followed him, somebody who was buying a white negligee."

Pat held up his hand. "That hasn't been proven."

"Screw the proof. Let's guess a little and see what we have. Now two things could have happened. Either the person Mitch saw and followed recognized him and backtracked Mitch to his apartment, or Mitch pulled a stupid trick. We know he tried to call Norm Harrison and missed him. We know he poked around in the morgue looking for a photo to confirm his suspicions. Supposing he decided to make a direct inquiry to the one he was after to bring him out into the open?"

"That's pretty damn dumb."

"Not if he thought the guy was too big to try the direct approach. He underestimated the opposition, but it could have paid off. Don't forget, he was waiting to see Norm Harrison. He could have expected it to be him at the door that night."

"And what have you got so far, Mike?"

"Everything's related so far. From the girls, to

Mitch, to Greta, to Gates, to Jones, to Ali Duval. It's stretching it pretty thin, but one thing holds it together . . . the thing that started the whole ball rolling . . . those negligees. If that one factor was removed, if those girls had been dressed differently, we never would have been where we are. That is, until Harry Service got into the act."

"Mike," Pat said seriously, "do you realize that we haven't anything tangible to go on? Take the guy you so nicely knocked off. . . ."

"And you get the other part of the picture," I said. "He had a contact with somebody in a big car. A chauffeur-driven one. Ali has a contact with someone in a big limousine. Now there's one thing that's been running throughout this business since I first got on it. I keep hearing the word gook kicked around. They told me that in the Village about Greta Service being seen with one. Jones calls Ali a gook. They called Orslo Bucher a gook. We have a foreign ship in port, Ali spotted by Jones as working some kind of racket and if it weren't for a couple of plain old American girls involved I'd say we had some kind of international intrigue going."

"You're going," Pat said. "You're not happy until you make a mess of everything."

"Yeah, then explain your interest in the way those girls died, old buddy. You were pretty sure you had something, or are you still on the sex-fiend kick?"

"It seems a little more logical than the web

you're trying to weave."

"Does it?"

Pat grimaced and filled the cups again. "Let me tell you something else, Mike. This afternoon we get another possible. You remember the Corning case about three years ago?"

"No."

"Well, it was kept pretty quiet. He committed six sex murders, all mutilations and pretty messy. He was caught and sent to a state institution for the criminally insane. After two and a half years of being a vegetable, he suddenly regained his senses and escaped. They got him in an abandoned house, but rather than surrender he burned the place down around himself. That's what they thought. There wasn't much of the corpse left to get a positive identification. This afternoon we get a call from someone who knew him well who said he saw Corning right here in the city. Now . . . if you want to know if I'm on a sex-fiend kick, maybe I am."

"You'll still keep Gates on the wanted sheet, though?"

"We can do that."

"What about the poison angle on the Poston kid?"

"The M.E. is making that his project. He's tracing sources. If something shows we'll follow that line too. Just so you can't say we're not covering every route I'll see what Interpol has on Ali Duval and have them pick up anybody in a fez who isn't a Shiner."

187

"What're you so nervous about, kid?" I grinned.

Pat gave me a pointed stare and said, "If you had those papers breathing down your neck the way I've had you would know why."

"You do it when a cop gets killed," I reminded him.

"That's different."

"Not for those guys. Besides, nothing's been printed yet."

"Only because they haven't turned up something either, but it's coming. If something doesn't break damn soon they'll cut loose at the department, then the action starts." He put his cup down on the table and tilted back in his chair. "Incidentally, your buddies with the papers put a squeeze on the D.A. All you'll be required to give in court is a reasonable explanation."

"Nice of them."

"Maybe they're just saving you to be a goat too in case it all falls apart."

"One goat's enough. I'll let it be you."

"Great. Thanks."

I grinned at him, slapped my hat on and said good night. He had enough troubles for one day.

When I got back to the hotel there were four messages in my box to call Velda at a number in Bradbury. I got up to the room, shucked my coat and had the operator put me through. The place was a motel outside of the town and her room didn't answer, so I said I'd call back and hung up.

I waited an hour and tried again. She still didn't answer so I lay back on the bed and snapped the light off.

At two-thirty she called me back, jarring me out of a sleep.

"Mike?"

"Here, kid. Go ahead."

"Look, I don't know whether this means anything or not, but this morning I made a contact in the bus station."

"Who was it?"

"Just a girl. She was in the ladies' room crying and I tried to find out what was wrong. When she finally got past the tears and started talking, she said she was stranded in town and had no way back to New York."

"Hell, that's a sucker story, honey. How many times . . . ?"

"Will you listen!" I lay back on the bed and told her to go ahead. She was always picking up wet birds in the street anyway. "I took her outside and bought her some coffee and let her spill it. She was brought out here last night by some man she met in a bar downtown when she was a little high. He said he was going to take her to a real party that would make New York look like a playground. On the drive out he said he worked at one of the embassy retreats and knew how they could look in on the whole show.

"Driving out she started to sober up and her new friend didn't look so good to her any more. His talk scared her to death. Twice he stopped

189

the car and tried to make a play for her, but both times other cars coming made him drive on. She fought him off, but couldn't get away. He kept telling her his boss really knew how to make a woman come around. All you had to do was hurt them enough and there wasn't anything they wouldn't do, anything at all. By this time she was nearly hysterical. He got to Bradbury, stopped for gas, but didn't have money to pay the attendant so he left his watch for security and said he'd pick it up tonight. That was as much as she heard. While he wasn't watching she got out of the car and ran for it, but she left her purse in the car and had no way to get it back."

"Didn't she ever hear of the Travelers Aid Society?" I said.

"Quit being funny," Velda told me. Her voice had an angry bite to it. "Anyway, I gave her fifteen dollars so she could get cleaned up — she spent the night sleeping in the bushes — and she was to meet me at the bus station later and point out the man when he came to reclaim his watch."

I nodded in the dark and said, "So you waited and waited and the little doll never showed up."

"No, she didn't."

"Kiss your fifteen bucks off, kitten."

"But I found the gas station she had mentioned. The guy had already reclaimed his watch. The attendant didn't know him, but verified the fact that he stopped there occasionally and apparently did work for one of the embassies because he used one of their cars on occasions."

Velda could have stumbled over something. I said, "What are the schedules out of there?"

"Three buses and two trains daily. I checked both places, but nobody answering her description bought a ticket. There was very little outbound traffic and she would have been spotted."

"Maybe she walked out a ways and flagged a bus down."

"I asked about that. They don't stop except for their regular stations."

"She could thumb," I suggested.

"Doubtful. There's an enforced law about that around here. Besides, after that one experience I don't think she'd want to lay herself open to another. My guess is that's she's still here in town. I'm going to canvass the resort area motels where they have off-season rentals and see if she checked into one of them. She was still shaken up and might not have wanted to travel in that condition. She had enough money for both her room and her fare besides."

"You get her name?"

"Certainly. Julie Pelham. I called the phone at her address and her landlady said she hadn't come in yet. She gave me a description that fit this girl but didn't seem too concerned about what had happened."

"Okay, check it out. Maybe you'll get your money back yet."

"One more thing, Mike," she said. "I asked around the local stores about the activities around the embassies. One of them has started laying in the usual supplies they get when a party's in the making. They spread it around trying to cover it up, but the signs are there."

"Which one?"

"I don't know yet. It isn't easy to get near those places. Besides their own security there are a lot of men in unmarked cars riding double around the area."

"They're our people."

"Yes, I know. They don't seem to like their jobs. What can you do with a crowd having diplomatic immunity?"

"Not much," I said, "so you forget that part and see if you can run down the girl. I'll check back with you tomorrow, so leave word for me. If you can't get to me, reach Pat or Hy."

"Suppose . . ."

"Don't suppose anything. Just do as I tell you to."

"Or what?"

I laughed into the phone. "I'll punch you right in the mouth with my lips."

"Hit me, man," she said and hung up.

I picked up the morning paper at the desk and flipped through the pages. There was a short piece inside about the police researching Mitch Temple's files to see if he had uncovered anything that might have led to his death and a short recap of his murder. Another mentioned that Maxine Delaney's death was still unsolved, but the police were expecting a break momentarily.

Nothing was said about Corning being at large, so Pat was probably keeping it squashed until it could be confirmed or the man apprehended. Most likely he had all available manpower out trying to track the guy down, but didn't release the information to the press to avert any panic. Most of the news was still political, split between the current foreign crisis and the last minute moves at the U.N. before the Assembly paused for a recess.

Hy's column mentioned that Dulcie McInnes had returned to town after a successful invasion of Washington and was resuming her position as unofficial hostess of New York's society set.

I tossed the paper down and called Hy's office. His secretary said he wasn't expected in for an hour, so I tried Al Casey, told him I wanted to see him and he said to come on up.

Al was curious about why I wanted to know the details of Gerald Ute's grand gesture of giving up his property in the Bradbury area to the various legations for recreational use, but didn't try to quiz me on it. He took me to the section smelling of old newsprint where they kept their clippings, found Ute's file and dragged it out.

Besides the news reports of the transaction, several of the columnists had discussed it, both pro and con, but nothing unfavorable went against Ute. The transfer did give him a tax break, but he was wealthy enough so that it didn't matter one way or another. Publicity wise, it gave him good coverage. His philanthropies covered a lot of angles and this was just another. There didn't appear to be any direction to his giveaway program, except that most of the causes seemed to be good ones and the grants justified.

The town of Bradbury wasn't pleased entirely — their local paper resented the intrusion of iron curtain members in their midst, but since other friendly members were represented in the grant, it could have been an all round show of good will.

I said, "Al, you been up to Bradbury?"

"When Ute opened the places I was. After that most of the places closed their gates. You know how these foreigners are. They don't want anybody prying around. As far as I know, everything's peaceful up there except when they bring in that jazz festival, but that's over on the beach section anyway."

"No rumors?"

He squinted at me, trying to fathom my meaning. "What are you getting at?"

"I don't know."

"Then there're no rumors. If there were any, we'd sure know about it. The locals up there will pick up any kind of gossip."

"Al," I said, "this Belar Ris . . . he's with the legation that uses one of those places up there, isn't he?"

"You know, Mike, that's the second time you brought that guy into it. Why?"

"Mitch took off on him in his column."

"I know. The guy's a modern day pirate, but so what? He's not the only one. That's the way they operate over there. The money boys run things so they can make more money. Mitch rapped him and others like him in his column, but that had been going on for a year. If Ris was going to move in on Mitch he'd buy the paper and fire him. Frankly, I don't think Ris gave a damn. He's still got diplomatic immunity."

Why was it that every time I heard those words something crawled up my back?

Al fingered through the file and pulled out an aerial photo of Gerald Ute's former estate. "Here's what interests you so much. Ten years ago he bought the old Davis-Clendenning property. It takes in about a thousand acres. What those fieldstone monstrosities represented to those two old men, I don't know, but they built a half dozen mansions around, rarely used them, then they were sold after they died. Ute picked it up, did some minor developing, couldn't find a use or a buyer for it and rather than let taxes chew him up, gave the place away. Over here is another section he donated to be used for civic affairs. That's where the jazz bash is held. He got a few others to chip in to build the amphitheater and practically finances the rest of the venture alone."

I wasn't interested in the jazz site. I said, "Which legation building is Ris associated with?"

Al scowled, looked at the photo and tapped the one in the northeast corner. "This one, I think. Hell, I don't remember." His eyes caught mine. "You got a lead on something?"

"An idea maybe," I said.

"Something we can help with?"

"Not yet."

"If it's got to do with Mitch, I'd like it now."

"You'll know about it if it does."

I left Al sitting there puzzled, then went downstairs and found a pay phone, dropped in a dime and dialed the Proctor Group number and asked for Dulcie. Miss Tabor let out another one of those horrified gasps, but put me through.

Dulcie McInnes came on with a pleasant laugh and said, "Mike, how nice. I was hoping you'd call."

"Me?"

"Yes, you. For some reason you seem to bring a little excitement into an otherwise staid life." Then she turned serious a moment with, "Mike . . . the girl we saw . . ."

"I notified her brother. That was all I could do. He wanted to be sure she was safe, that's all."

"Well, it sure caused a flurry around here. Do you know the police have been here inquiring about Teddy Gates?"

"What about him?"

"I don't know. Nobody knows where he is. He isn't at home and he hasn't shown up at work. I wish you'd tell me what's going on."

"He may be caught in the middle of a big one,"

I said. "If he's found he'll supply a lot of answers."

For a second she didn't say anything, but I could hear her steady breathing. "Mike . . . can this hurt the Proctor Group? You know, will there be any publicity?"

"I don't see how. If he was engaged in something outside the office it shouldn't touch you."

"Please, Mike. Be sure. If they find out . . . well, even though I helped you . . . the Board certainly won't like it. I can't afford to be involved in anything sensational and neither can the magazine."

"We can keep a lid on it. Look . . . can I see you again?"

"I'd love to, Mike. When?"

"As soon as possible. I want you to exert a little of your influence for me."

"Oh?"

"I want to meet Belar Ris."

Her laughter was a clear tinkle. "Social climber," she told me. "I should think you could do better. Now there are several young ladies of respectable and wealthy parents who . . ."

"I'm not kidding, Dulcie. Can it be arranged?"

She caught the imperativeness in my voice and got serious again. "Do you have a black tie?"

"I'll get one."

"Tonight there's a reception at the Flamingo Room for one of the delegations. Mr. Ris will be there. I'm invited and I'll be happy to have you escort me. Suppose you meet me at seven-thirty

197

in the lobby. Now, can you tell me why?"

"Later."

"Mike . . ."

"What?"

"If you hear anything about Teddy Gates . . ."

"Don't worry, he'll turn up. I'll make sure we keep a lid on it."

"Thank you, Mike."

"See you tonight."

When I hung up I waited a few seconds, then tried the number in Bradbury that Velda had given me. There was no answer in her room and no messages for me either.

I tried Pat and got him in. He told me he had to go uptown and to meet him at the Blue Ribbon in an hour.

New York was still under its blanket of gray. There was a damp, clammy chill in the air and the streets were devoid of their usual crowds. I had forty-five minutes to waste, so I headed west, taking it easy, and got to the Blue Ribbon in time to have coffee with George before Pat got there. He came in exactly on schedule, tossed his hat on the rack and pulled out a chair opposite me. He looked tired, tiny lines pulling at the corner of his eyes and mouth.

He waited until his own coffee came before he said, "The Corning deal washed out."

"What happened?"

"We picked up the guy in the neighborhood he was spotted in. It was one of those damn look-alike situations and I couldn't blame the guy who fingered him. He was pretty indignant, but played the good citizen bit and even let us print him for a positive I.D. The guy was clean . . . service record in Washington, executive job in Wall Street for fifteen years. A real bust."

"Scratch one sex fiend."

"There's something else." Pat reached into his pocket and pulled out two folded white sheets and handed them to me. There was a peculiar look in his eyes and he edged forward in his chair. "Our M.E. ferreted this out. Remember me telling you about chemical substitutes that induce the same symptoms he found in the Poston girl?"

I nodded.

"There's the formula. The stuff isn't even produced in this country at all. It's made in limited quantities by a French firm and distributed to selected outlets that use the stuff for chemical analysis tests in locating certain rare elements in earth samples. One of those buyers is Pericon Chemicals."

I looked up from the report and felt my eyes start to narrow. "Ronald Miller, Mitch Temple's friend. He's with them."

"Yeah, his army buddy, the book writer."

"We got hold of him this morning," Pat told me. "He confirmed the use of this product . . . called it C-130 . . . and even knew of its side effects. In fact, its properties are clearly stated on the containers. Before they handled it properly, the stuff killed a lot of people by being induced through skin abrasions. It's been manufactured since 1949 and a record is kept of its sales and use.

"Now here comes the kicker. A year ago part of an order going to Pericon Chemicals was stolen in shipment. None of it has ever been recovered, although the manufacturers conducted an exhaustive search and even issued notices as to its deadly effects. A check with the company showed that two previous inquiries had been made to them requesting a sale of the product, but were turned down because they only sell to specific companies for specific purposes. Both inquiries were by phone. And now here it is — that C-130 was being shipped on board the *Pinella* on a trip from Marseilles to Tangiers."

"Ali Duval," I hissed.

"He was a steward on the ship then too."

"There's a weak point there, Pat."

"I know," he said. "Mitch Temple didn't know for sure how the Poston girl might have died. He had no reason to check with Miller on that angle."

"He wanted something, *that's* for sure," I said.

Pat nodded. "Pericon Chemicals got involved in some litigation over the theft and we're going into that for what it's worth. There's got to be some connection."

"How expensive is that stuff?"

"It sells for twelve hundred dollars an ounce."

"That's more than H."

"And a half liter is missing."

I let out a low whistle. "That's a lot of loot. Somebody was still taking a chance on handling it."

"The package wouldn't be very large. It could be moved around. Hell, the stuff is even soluble in water and can be impregnated into clothes and recovered later the same way."

"No sign of Ali Duval?"

"Nothing yet. He was of French Arabian parentage and we're covering all the places he might go to find his own kind. Photos of Duval are being circulated and if he's around, we'll find him."

"And charge him with what?"

"We'll break him down."

"I didn't ask that."

"That's the other hole in the picture. I'd rather not think about it right now. If he's wrapped up in anything, maybe another country will want to pick him up. The inquiry to Interpol is out now and I'm waiting for an answer." Pat paused and finished his coffee. He put the cup down carefully, his eyes watching my face. "Have you got anything more to add?"

"Not yet."

He would have known if I were lying. He nodded and said, "I'm going to check a couple of belly dance places tonight. Native music . . . the real stuff they say. Want to tag along?"

"Not tonight. I got a date."

"Better than a belly dancer?"

I looked at him with a slow grin. "Much."

Pat felt in his pocket, extracted a two-by-two photo and tossed it on the table. "Here's a passport telephoto of your boy Duval. You might want to know what he looks like."

I said thanks and Pat walked off. I looked at the picture, studying the ineptitude of some photographer. The telephoto process and subsequent reproduction had modified the features, taking out the sharpness of the original photo, but Duval was still distinguishable. He was a tanned face with nothing spectacular about him until you saw the eyes and the innate savagery that lay behind them.

chapter ten

The curb in front of the hotel on Park Avenue was lined with limousines. Photographers roamed the sidewalks, picking their way through the curious, trying for a spot to snap the greats of the international set for their society pages.

Most of the cars were chauffeur-driven, and pulled away after discharging their passengers, but another group bearing DPL plates parked wherever they wanted to, insolently occupying the space in the no-parking zones. Two mounted cops on horseback disgustedly ignored them and concentrated on keeping traffic moving the best they could.

I got out of my cab and went into the lobby past one of the photographers who looked at me uncertainly a second before he spotted someone he was sure of. I stood in line, checked my hat and coat, then drifted off looking for Dulcie. From any side except the front, most of the males were indistinguishable in their identical tuxedos, but the women stood out in the plumage and I wondered what the hell ever happened to the order of things. In nature, the males wore the gaudy colors and the females were the drab ones.

You could tell the pecking order of this barn-yard by the preferential treatment accorded the greater luminaries. They were fawned upon, deferred to and waited on incessantly, always surrounded by their retinue. The babble of sound was punctuated by foreign tongues and the shrill laughter of the women, stuffy animals who strutted for the benefit of anyone who would look.

This is society, I thought. Brother.

Some of them had already formed their little coalitions and were drifting toward the elevators, deep in conversation, the women trailing behind them, their attitudes artificial, their posturing inane. There were some who had the earmarks of complacency and I figured them for either the genuine articles, born to build and control empires, or those who just didn't give a damn.

A couple of times I caught sight of myself in one of the mirrors and I looked uncomfortably out of place. Twice, men I cased as security personnel went by and we nodded imperceptibly. I was being taken for one of their own and their eyes didn't miss the way the jacket was tailored to conceal a gun or the mark of the professional any more than my own did.

At seven-thirty Dulcie arrived with several others, made her rounds of formal cheek-kissing and handshaking, but all the while searched the faces around her for me. I waved, let her get done with it all, check her wrap, then walked over trying not to grin like an idiotic schoolkid.

Dulcie wasn't the peacock type at all. Her gown was a black sheath that fitted as though there was nothing beneath it at all. Her hair was up in a mass of soft waves with lights bouncing off the silver accents like an electrical display. There was a diamond necklace at her throat and a thin diamond bracelet watch on her wrist.

But she was the most striking thing there.

I said, "Hello, beautiful."

Her fingers grabbed my hand and she tilted her head back and laughed softly. "That's not a proper society salutation, big man."

"It was the only thing I could think of."

"You did fine," she said and squeezed my fingers. "I like." She ran her eyes up and down me and said with approval, "You make quite a figure in that tux."

"Only for you, baby. I'm not a clothes horse."

"That's what I thought. I was afraid you might not come."

"Wouldn't miss it for the world. I could use exposure to some of the nicer things in life."

Dulcie threw me a tilted glance. "Don't expect too much. Some of these people come from strange corners of the world. It's still rough out there." She hooked her arm under mine. "Shall we go up to the Flamingo Room?"

"That's what we came for," I said. We started in the direction of the elevators, mingling with the others. While we waited I asked her, "Anything new on Gates?"

"No. One of the other boys took over his appointments. He's left quite a gap in things. Mike . . . what do you think happened to him?"

"If I knew I'd be making him spill his guts out. He's got himself in some kind of bind and is riding it out."

"I went to the trouble of calling the agencies who give him assignments. He isn't out on any of theirs. What he had to do was either for us or for himself in his own studio. One of his friends had a key to his apartment and inventoried his equipment. He didn't take anything with him at all."

"He won't get far."

Dulcie shook her head, her face thoughtful. "I don't know. Matt Prince who does our developing and Teddy were pretty close. He said Teddy kept a lot of money in his office desk. It isn't there now."

"How much?"

"Over a thousand dollars. He was always buying new cameras or lenses. Matt said Teddy never worried about leaving it around. He had plenty of money anyway."

"He could go a long way on a grand."

The elevator came before she could answer me and we stepped back in the car. Going up Dulcie introduced me to a few of the others there who looked at me strangely, not sure who I could be, but certain I must have some importance since I was with her.

The Flamingo Room was a burst of color and noise when we walked into it, a montage of patterns made up of people in motion, under the flags of all the nations that dangled from the ceiling, waving in idle motion under the pressure of some unseen breeze. An orchestra was at the rear, varying its selections to suit every national taste, and tables were arranged around the sides piled with delicacies from countless countries. Champagne corks popped constantly and the clink of hundreds of glasses punctuated the hum of voices.

"What ever happened to the poverty program?" I asked her.

She poked me and said, "Hush!" with a stifled laugh.

Dulcie had an incredible memory for names, even the tongue twisters. She mingled easily, the right words always ready, her capacity for pleasing others absolutely incredible. More than one man looked at me enviously for being her escort, trying to catalogue me in their minds.

When I had to I could play the game too. It didn't come as easily and began to wear thin after the first hour. I hadn't come to hobnob and Dulcie sensed my irritation and suggested a cocktail at the bar.

We had just started toward it when Dulcie said casually, "There's Belar Ris," and swerved toward one corner of the room where three men were grouped, talking.

One dog can always tell another dog. They can see them, smell them, or hear them, but they never mistake them for anything but another dog. They can be of any size, shape or color, but a dog is a dog to a dog.

Belar Ris stood with his back angled to the wall. To an indifferent observer he was simply in idle conversation, but it wasn't like that at all. This was an instinctive gesture of survival, being in constant readiness for an attack. His head didn't turn and his eyes didn't seem to move, but I knew he saw us. I could feel the hackles on the back of my neck stiffening and knew he felt the same way.

Dog was meeting dog. Nobody knew it but the dogs and they weren't telling.

He was bigger than I thought. The suggestion of power I had seen in his photographs was for real. When he moved it was with the ponderous grace of some jungle animal, dangerously deceptive, because he could move a lot faster if he had to.

When we were ten feet away he pretended to see us for the first time and a wave of charm washed the cautious expression from his face and he stepped out to greet Dulcie with outstretched hand.

But it wasn't her he was seeing. It was me he was watching. I was one of his own kind. I couldn't be faked out and wasn't leashed by the proprieties of society. I could lash out and kill as fast as he could and of all the people in the room, I was the potential threat. I knew what he felt because I felt the same way myself.

He had the skin coloration of one of the Mediterranean groups. His eyes were almost black under thick, black brows that swept to a V over a hawklike nose that could have had an Arabian origin. Pomaded hair fitted like a skullcap and his teeth were a brilliant white in the slash of his smile.

Dulcie said, "Mr. Ris, how nice to see you. May I present Mr. Hammer?"

For the first time he looked directly at me and held out his hand. His forearm that protruded from his jacket sleeve showed no cuff and I knew I had been right. Even under a tux he wore a short-sleeved shirt.

"Delighted, Mr. Hammer." His voice was accented and deep, but devoid of any of the pleasure his smile feigned.

"Good to see you, Mr. Ris." The handshake was brief and hard.

"And are you a member of our great United Nations group? I don't remember having seen you. . . ."

I wasn't going to play games with him. "Hell, no," I said. "I'm a private cop."

For a split second there was a change in his eyes, a silent surprise because I couldn't be bothered acting a part. For Dulcie's sake he played it with an even bigger smile and said, "I certainly approve. Anyone as charming as Miss McInnes certainly needs a protector. But here, my dear, as if there was any danger . . ." He let his sentence drift and glanced at me questioningly.

"Half these people here are fighting one another a few thousand miles away," I said.

Belar Ris wouldn't drop his smile. "Ah, yes,

but here we are making peace. Is that not so?"

"That'll be the day," I said. I knew what my face looked like. I wore my own kind of grin that happened automatically when an enemy was in front of me and felt my eyes in a half squint and a funny relaxed feeling across my chest.

"You are not one of those who have confidence in the United Nations then, Mr. Hammer. That is too bad. It is such a monument to . . . to . . ." He paused, searching for words. "The integrity of the world."

I said, "Bullshit."

"Mike!" Dulcie's face had turned pink and she nudged me with her elbow. "What a terrible thing to say."

"Ask the boys who were in Korea or Viet Nam or Stanleyville. Ask . . ."

Belar Ris threw his head back and let out a deep chuckle. "That is perfectly all right, Mr. Hammer. You see, it is people like you who must be convinced, then you will be the most firm advocates of the united world. It will take much discussion, many arguments and positive persuasions before things are resolved." He held out his hand to me again. "Good evening, Mr. Hammer." His fingers tightened deliberately and I threw everything I had into the grip. I could do it that way too. He felt me buck him, then let my hand go. "It is a good thing to have the opinion of . . . the man on the street," he said. He nodded to Dulcie, gave her a small bow that was typically European. "Miss McInnes."

He walked away, his blocky figure the picture of confidence. Dulcie watched him a moment, then turned to me. "Is that what you came for? If I thought it was to get in a political argument . . . You embarrassed him!"

"Did I?"

Then she let the laugh go, trying to stifle it with a hand. "It was funny. Even when you said that awful word."

"So wash my mouth out with soap."

"Really, Mike. Now can you tell me why you wanted to meet him?"

"You wouldn't understand, kid."

"Are you . . . satisfied?"

I took her arm and steered her toward the bar. "Perfectly," I said. "Someplace in the pattern there's a place for him."

"You're talking in riddles. Let's have our drink and you can take me home. I have a big weekend with a new issue of the magazine in front of me and can't afford any late nights until it's put to bed."

"That's too bad," I said.

Her fingers tightened on my arm. "I know." She rubbed her head against my shoulder. "There will be other times."

I left Dulcie outside her apartment and told the cab driver to take me back to my hotel. Upstairs, I got out of my tux, mixed myself a drink and slouched in a chair with my feet on the window sill, looking out at the night.

Sometime not too long ago a point had been reached and a bridge crossed. It was too dark to see the outlines of it, but I could feel it and knew it was there. Too long that little thing had been gnawing at the corners of my mind and I tried to sift it out, going over the puzzle piece by piece. One word, one event, could change the entire course of the whole thing. Out there on the streets Pat and his men and the staff of the paper were scouring the city for that one thing too. Somebody had to find it. I finished my drink, made another and was halfway through it when my phone rang. It was my answering service for the office number with the message that I had several calls from the same number and the party gently insisted that they were urgent.

I dialed the number, heard it ring, then Cleo's voice said, "Mike Hammer?"

"Hello, Cleo."

"You never came back."

"I would have."

"You'd better come now," she said.

"Why?"

"Because I know something you'd like to know." There was a lilt to her voice as if she had been belting a few drinks.

"Can't you tell me now?"

"Nope. I'm going to tell you when you get here." She laughed gently and put the phone back. I said something under my breath and redialed her number. It rang a dozen times but she wouldn't answer it. I cradled the receiver, then got up and climbed into my clothes. It was eleven-thirty and one hell of a time to be starting out again.

There are times when something happens to Greenwich Village. It gives a spasmodic heave as if trying for a rebirth and during its convulsions the people who dwell in her come out to watch the spectacle. It's hard to tell whether it's the inanimate old section or the people themselves, but you know that something is happening. Windows that never show light suddenly brighten; figures who have merely been shadows in doorways take life and move. There is an influx from neighboring parts, people being disgorged from taxicabs to be swallowed up again in the maw of the bistros whose mouths are open wide to receive them.

The peculiar ones with the high falsettos, skin-tight pants and jackets tossed over shoulders capelike display themselves for public viewing, pleased that they are the center of attraction, each one trying for the center of the spotlight. Their counterparts, sensing new prey available, ready themselves, then stalk toward their favorite hunting grounds, masculine in their movements, realizing that sooner or later someone will respond to the bait being cast out, then the slow, teasing struggle would begin, and they, being the more wise, would make the capture.

A sureness seemed to be the dominant attitude. Everybody seemed so sure of themselves for that one single night. The heavy damp that should have been oppressive worked in reverse, a challenge to stay outside and dare the elements, a reason to go indoors to expend the excessive energy that was suddenly there.

I got out of the cab on Seventh Avenue and walked through the crowds, watching them pulsate across the streets at the change of the lights, feeling the static charge of their presence. I wasn't part of them at all and it was as though I were invisible. They had direction of purpose, to be part of the pleasure of the rebirth. I had direction of course only and picked my way to the house where Greta Service had lived and pushed Cleo's bell.

The buzzer clicked on the lock and I went inside, let the door shut behind me and went up the stairs to the top floor and stood there in the dark. I didn't knock. She knew I was there. I waited a minute, then her door opened silently, flooding the landing with a soft rose glow from the lights behind her and she was wearing one of those things you could see through again.

"Hello, Mike."

I walked inside, let her take my hat and coat from me and picked up the drink she had waiting on top of the table. Her project had been finished and her work area was rearranged, her tools and equipment placed to become part of the decorative concept of the room. Through the skylight and the full French windows I could see the outline of New York above the opaque surfaces of buildings around her.

"Pensive tonight, aren't you?" She went over and pulled a cord, then another, closing out the view through the windows. It was like pulling the covers over your head in bed.

"Sorry," I said.

"No need to be. You'll loosen up. Even if I make you."

"It's one of those nights," I told her.

"I know. You felt it too, didn't you?"

I nodded.

She walked past me, the sheer nylon of the full-length housecoat crackling, the static making it cling to her body like another skin. She switched the record player on and let Tchaikovsky's *Pathétique* seep into the room. She turned, swirling the ice in the glass in her hand as the subtle tones began their journey into life. "Fitting music, isn't it?"

I looked at her and tasted my drink. She had built it just right.

"They don't know it out there," she said. "They take time out of their expressionless little existences trying to find something vital here and leave things as they found them. They really go away empty."

"What did you have to tell me, Cleo?"

She smiled, crossed one arm under her breasts, balanced the other on it and sipped her drink. "But you aren't one of them."

"Cleo . . ."

She paid no attention to me. She walked up, took the drink I didn't know I had finished from my hand very slowly and went and made me another. "Do you remember what I told you when you were here?"

"No."

"I said I wanted to paint you."

"Look . . ."

"Specially now." Her eyes viewed me with an odd interest. She turned her head from side to side, moved to study me in a different light, then said, "Yes, something has happened to you since the last time. It's better now. Like it should be. There isn't any softness at all left."

I put the drink down and she shook her head very gently. "It's something you want to know, Mike, but you'll have to do what I want you to do first."

I said, "I found Greta."

"Good," she said, and smiled again. "It's more than that now though, isn't it?"

"Come on, Cleo. What have you got on your mind?"

She walked up to me, turned her back and took my hands, wrapping them around her waist. Her hair brushed my face and it smelled faintly of a floral scent. "I work for the Proctor Group too, or have you forgotten? I knew when you went up to see Dulcie McInnes. You should never have said what you did to her Miss Tabor. That old harridan can't stand dominant males."

"I was there," I admitted.

She turned in my arms, her body a warm thing against mine. "And I was jealous." She smiled,

216

let her arms crawl up my sides, her hands going to my face, then lacing them behind my head. "I saw you first," she grinned. "Am I teasing well enough?"

"I'm hurting. Don't lean on me too hard."

"There was some strange speculation about Teddy Gates. Now he's missing after you paid another visit up there. People are talking, yet nobody really knows anything at all."

"Except you."

"Except me," she repeated. "You found Greta Service, but it couldn't have ended because you're here now to find out something else."

I ran my fingers down the small of her back and felt her body arch under them. "What's your price, Cleo?"

"You," she said. "I'm going to paint you first. I want you permanently inscribed so I can look at you and touch you and talk to you whenever I want and know you'll never fade away." She raised herself on her toes and her mouth touched mine lightly. Then she let herself down and pushed away from me, her eyes sad little imps dancing in far off places.

"I'm a funny woman, Mike. I'm young-old. I've seen too much and done too much in too short a time. What I really want I can never have, but I have sense enough to realize it, so I take what I can get when I can get it, or is that too complicated?"

"I understand."

"This is Cleo's last stand here." She swept her

arm around to take in the room. "It's very little, but it's a sanctuary of a sort. From here I can see the other part of the world and nobody can touch me. I can stay here forever and ever with all the good parts of me right where I want them, never changing, never turning their backs. Do I sound too philosophical?"

"You can do better."

The imps in her eyes danced again. "But I don't want to. I'm alive here, Mike. Now I'm going to make you part of that life. I won't sell you. I won't give you away. I'm going to keep you. You're going to be mine like nobody else ever had you."

"Cleo . . ."

"Or what you want to know won't be yours."

I put the drink down. "Your show, kid. Do I loosen my tie?"

"You take off your clothes, Mike."

She painted me that night. It wasn't what I had expected. The background was a jungle green with little bright blobs of orange that seemed to explode outward from the canvas, distorting the sensation of seeing a flat surface. There was a man in the picture and it was me, but not so much the physical representation as the mental one. It was the id rather than the ego, the twilight person you were only when you had to be. She had seen things and caught them, registering them for all time as we know it and when I saw myself as she did it was the same as looking at the face of an enemy. The short hairs on the back of my neck raised in sudden anger at the confrontation and I knew what Belar Ris had seen just as I had seen him. My .45 was there too, exact in detail almost to seeming three-dimensional, but it was away from my hands as if I didn't need it.

During the hours she had discarded the sheer nylon, working unfettered, concentrating solely on the portrait. I could study her abstractly, enjoying the loveliness of her body, then in the stillness my mind had drifted to other things and Cleo was only a warm outline of motion, of long smooth sweeps of pink, blossoming mounds that were half hidden behind the easel, then quickly there again. I had time to think in an unreal world where thinking was all there was to do. The extended strands of the web began to join together with the cross sections of odd conjecture, and little by little, piece by piece, the thing that was possible became probable.

She let me have that one brief look, then turned the canvas to face the wall.

"You're mine now," she said. Her finger touched a switch and the lights faded gradually into nothingness and the two of us were there alone, people again, barely visible, whitish silhouettes against the velvet of night.

Behind the curtains a false dawn marked the beginning of a new day. The spasm outside was over and whether the Village was in the agony of rebirth or the throes of death, I would never know. We had bought the hours at a price. We

219

had spent excesses we had accumulated during that time, and for a little while there was that crazy release that was a climax and an anticlimax that left no time for work or thought any more.

I looked at the day crawling through the skylight. She had pulled back the blinds so that the glass was a huge square of wet gray overhead, wiggling with wormy raindrops that raced to the bottom to form a pool before dripping off the edge of the sill.

I rolled off the couch and reached for my clothes. I could smell the aroma of coffee as I got dressed and called for her twice without getting an answer. I dressed quickly, found an electric percolator bubbling in the kitchen, poured myself a cup hurriedly and swallowed it down.

Then I saw her note.

It was written in charcoal on a sketching pad, just a few lines, but it said enough.

Mike Darling . . . the man Sol Renner saw Greta with has his picture in the paper beneath. Thank you for everything, it was lovely. You'll never leave me now.

Good-by, Cleo.

I yanked the paper out from under the pad. It was the same copy Biff had shoved under my nose the other night. The man in the picture was Belar Ris.

The web was pulling tighter, but I still couldn't see the spider. I put my hat on and went back through the studio. The easel was still in place, but the picture was gone. The place still smelled of her perfume and the nylon thing was lying across the back of the chair. *Pathétique* was still playing, the record never having been rejected.

She had chosen a good piece. Symphony No. 6 in B minor, Opus 74. Tchaikovsky should have stuck around to write another. This one would be even better.

chapter eleven

I stopped by the hotel, showered and changed into fresh clothes. No calls had come in and when I phoned Velda's number there was no answer and no messages. I left word for her to call me as soon as she arrived and dialed Pat. The desk sergeant told me he had left an hour ago and hadn't reported in yet, but had asked if I had tried to contact him. I thanked him and hung up softly though I felt like slamming the receiver back on the cradle.

I called Hy's office and that didn't answer.

Dulcie's phone didn't answer either, then I remembered it was Saturday. Modern technology had given us two days of rest. I got so damn disgusted I went downstairs to the lobby and picked up a copy of the paper and flipped through it without really seeing anything until I came to the center fold.

Somebody had snapped a shot of Belar Ris, Dulcie and me talking, but my back was to the camera and all you could see was Dulcie and Belar Ris and it looked for all the world as if we were enjoying ourselves.

I threw the paper on a chair and was about to go out when the desk clerk stopped me. I wasn't signed in under my right name, but he knew the room I was in and pointed to a row of phones against the wall. I picked it up and said, "Yeah?"

"Mike?"

"Speaking."

"Pat. What's got hold of you?"

"Listen . . ."

"You listen. Meet me at the Blue Ribbon about six-thirty. Have you called Hy?"

"He wasn't in. Why?"

"Because they found Gates," he said. "Some tramp tripped over the body under a culvert that goes over the Belt Parkway. Gates shoved a .22 pistol in his mouth and pulled the trigger, or at least that's the way it looked. He's been dead since the day he left according to the M.E.'s estimate on the spot."

"Where does Hy fit in?"

"Tell him to squash the story until we can move on it."

"The last time I tried that Mitch got killed."

"Mike . . ."

"Okay. I'll leave word. Just one thing . . . did he have any money on him?"

"Damn right, almost nine hundred bucks in cash."

"He didn't get very far," I said.

"What?"

"Nothing. I'll see you at six-thirty."

Now Gates, I thought. That opens the web again, but just a little bit. The spider was still inside.

Pat was late. I sweated him out for an hour,

playing with the coffee George had sent up to the table. Outside, the rain blasted down with the furious derision nature can have for humans, laughing at the futile attempts people put up to avoid her.

Pat finally came in whipping the rain from his hat, one of the young lawyers from the District Attorney's staff behind him. He introduced him quickly as Ed Walker and they sat down opposite me. Walker was looking at me as if I were a specimen in a zoo and I felt like slamming him one.

Pat said, "Reach Hy?"

"I told you I'd leave word. It was the best we can do."

"Good enough."

"Why?"

"The county police accepted Gates' death as suicide. We're not sure. How'd you tap the money angle?"

I told him what Dulcie had mentioned to me.

"That might figure in."

"Pat," I said, "don't get lost in this. A guy with a grand in his pocket doesn't knock himself off without a big run first."

"That's what I mean," he told me. "Any coroner's jury would direct a verdict of suicide the way it was set up. He used his own gun, even the cartridges and the clip had his fingerprints on it and there was a possible motive behind his own death."

I pushed my coffee away and flipped a butt between my lips. "Get to it."

"Tell him, Ed."

Walker opened his briefcase, took out several sheets of paper and referred to them. He looked at Pat, then me, shrugged once and laid them flat on the table. "You guys have the screwiest deal I ever saw."

"He's been in this from the beginning."

"But I haven't. Damn, my curiosity is worse than a cat's and someday it's going to get me the same thing."

Pat said annoyed, "Come on, Ed."

Walker nodded and adjusted his notes. "I pushed a few people overseas and got the details of the litigation the Pericon Chemical Company hit the steamship line with concerning the theft of that C-130. During the hassle the Pericon people uncovered the true owners of the shipping line. The majority control belonged to Belar Ris."

I said, "Oh?" and wondered why it came out so casually.

Pat's eyes were all over me, picking me apart. "That isn't the end of it. I have the report from Interpol. Ali Duval has been associated with Belar Ris since the late forties. He started off as an Algerian terrorist fighting the French, was picked up by Ris somewhere along the line and used by him as an enforcer in several of his enterprises. Duval is suspected of having committed nine different murders and an assault on a political personage from Aden. We might be able to get him held on the last charge. Once they get him in their hands they'll make him talk. It's a lousy way of doing things, but a threat to turn him over to them might work wonders."

"You're sure you can nail him then?"

"He'll leave on the *Pinella*."

"Where is he now?"

"Nobody seems to know," Pat said.

"And Ris?"

"He's had a tap on his phone for the last twelve hours. We know where he is." Pat gave me a laconic grin and said, "He called your erstwhile friend Dulcie McInnes at three-fifteen this afternoon and confirmed his appointment to pick her up for some affair they're having out at the estate in Bradbury this evening. We're going to cover that place like the lid on a pan tonight and if Duval shows we'll nail him."

"What about Ris?"

"Those damn dipples can get away with murder and we can't do a thing about it."

"Those what?"

"Dipples," Pat repeated. "DPL plates. Diplomatic immunity. He'll get away clear until he's declared *persona non grata* and tries to re-enter the country."

And there it was. The guy Mitch Temple chased who could get away with speeding on the Belt Parkway while he got stopped in the cab. The guy who made the contact with Orslo Bucher. The guy in the black official limousine who dropped Ali Duval off. Damn, it was there all the time. The *dipple* car. *Old Greenie had even called it that!*

I got up without saying anything and went to the wall phone and dropped in a dime. I gave the operator Velda's number. The manager of the motel said she hadn't returned to her room, but if I was to call to tell me that the answer was in Bradbury and she was going inside to get her fifteen dollars back. She'd be at G-14. The guy sounded puzzled.

The phone almost fell from my fingers. I wanted to yell, "No, don't try it alone" — but nobody would have heard me.

I didn't bother to pick up my coat. George didn't question me, but just gave me the keys to his car when I asked for them and I went out the front way leaving Pat and Walker still sitting there waiting for me, got the car out of the garage and headed out of the city.

Saturday was just another night in Bradbury. Two hours from New York put it another world away in another dimension. I stopped at a gas station on the edge of town, filled the tank and had the attendant point out the direction of the former Gerald Ute estate. In twenty minutes I reached the edge of the area he described to me, a rise in the road that gave a panoramic view of the landscape below.

Here and there in the distance lights winked between the trees, and when I had them located, drove past them. Every so often another car would pass going in the opposite direction, and once one drew abreast of me while the occupant scrutinized my face, then sped ahead and cut off at a side road.

Our people, I was thinking. The whole place was under constant surveillance. They'd keep up a running conversation on their car radios to keep me spotted until they were sure I had left their section. George's car didn't have DPL plates. There would be other security if I could get inside their compounds that would be even tighter. How did Velda think she could make it?

I circled the whole region until I came back to the outskirts of the city. There wasn't one way of telling just where the hell she was! Those buildings were scattered in haphazard fashion behind their towering walls and if I tried them one at a time I could be too late.

But what was it the guy had said on the phone? Velda would be at G-14. She'd expect me to know what that was. She had more sense than to try and hit a target like that by herself. The message wouldn't be too cryptic. It would be something I should recognize.

It was. It took me long enough to get it. I found a service station that I generally used, went in and got one of their standard road maps of the local area and looked at the grid markings on the side. The point where the vertical G and horizontal 14 intersected was two miles from my present position. I thanked the guy, got behind the wheel and turned around.

There were no lights showing in the building at all, but there was the barest reflection from the chrome trim of the cars that were parked in front of it to tell me it was far from deserted. I had run George's car into the brush beside the wall, nosing it in far enough so as to be practically invisible from the side road I had turned onto. From the roof I was able to reach the top of the wall and pull myself up. I flattened out, getting my eyes adjusted to the darkness, then swung over and dropped to the ground. Now I was thankful for the rain we had had. The bush I hit crumpled wetly, rather than crackling under the impact. I stood there fighting the urge to run, the .45 in my hand, the hammer back.

It was almost too quiet and that eerie stillness saved my neck. I heard the whispering thud of feet, the breath and the guttural snarl the same second I ducked to one side and felt something brush my arm and heard the wicked snap of teeth closing on air. The dog's leap took him into the same bush I had landed on, but to him it was more of an obstacle. I could see him then, clawing to break loose from the entangling branches, a sleek muscular killer, attack-trained to kill silently and quickly in the dark.

I whipped the .45 down across his head, saw him sag, recover, then go down again the second time when the muzzle of the gun smashed his skull. There would be more than one dog on the premises. They'd be like sentinels making their rounds. The others hadn't gotten the smell of me yet, and when they did, would come in almost silently and unseen like the other one.

I stayed close to the tree line, ran across the open lawn to the parking area and lost myself in the dozen or so cars parked beside the house for a few minutes, trying to figure a way in. As near as I was I could see the vague outlines of the windows and the lights that filtered past drawn curtains.

The main entrance was to my left, but I didn't want to hit the doors. Those would be well guarded. The larger windows that opened on the main rooms wouldn't be any good either. I didn't know what I was going into and had to feel my way there.

I could see the place now. It was built in a Victorian style of native brick and looked like a great stone fortress. But all fortresses had chinks and this one was in its style of architecture. The gingerbread ornaments that littered its face made perfect handholds. I shoved the .45 back in the sling, edged to the side of the building and began climbing.

Twenty feet up I had almost reached the second level. Down below I heard a snarl of impatience, then a door opened and a shaft of light illuminated the front of the building. Another dog, a huge Doberman, padded by, stood in the light a moment sniffing the air, then a voice said, "What is it?"

Another one answered with, "Nothing. They are always like that."

The door closed and the night took back its own. The dog snarled again, but from another point this time.

I didn't take any chances with the windows. The odds were that they had alarms rigged to them. I kept climbing until I felt the cornice of the roof under my hands and wiggled myself over the top. I lay there and looked at the ground a long way below, and when I was satisfied no one had seen me, picked my way to the cupola that sat like a silly little hat right in the middle of the building.

They hadn't bothered to wire these windows. I leaned my elbow against one until it gave, shattered gently and fell inside with a noisy tinkle, then picked out the larger pieces, opened the catch and swung it in on its rusted hinges.

No practical purpose was served by the cupola. It was dirty and empty, just the remnant of an era long past. I found the stairwell leading down, cupped a lit match in my hand and went down to the door. It had a large, old-fashioned latch that moved easily when I lifted it, and when I pushed against the door it swung out without a sound.

I was on the third level of the building in a corridor dimly lit from the light that rose from an open staircase at the far end. A series of rooms led off the hall, four on each side. I tried a couple of the doors, smelled the mustiness and dust that oozed out of the rooms and knew they weren't used. At one time they were probably designed for servants' quarters and had been vacant a long time.

From below I could hear the sound of voices

231

and I followed the hall to the staircase and looked around it. There was a landing below, a ninety degree bend in the stairs and nothing was visible. I started down the first step, saw the small movement of a shadow on the wall beneath me and drew my foot back. They had that area covered by a guard.

Several times when I was a kid I had been in old houses like these and I remembered that they generally had a service exit to the other floors for the servants. I went back down the hall, around the bend and found what I was looking for. The steps were old and dry and creaked under my feet, so I stayed as close to the wall as I could get. I made it to the second level and pushed the door open.

This time I almost wasn't lucky at all. The man sitting there with his chair tilted back against the wall tried to come to his feet and reach for the gun in his belt at the same time. The movement was too sudden and the chair slid out from under him. Even then he almost had time. He rolled, pulled the gun and was bringing it up when my toe caught him under the chin and almost took his head off. His jaw was tilted at a wild angle, his bottom teeth cutting into his cheek. His eyes were wide open, but he wasn't seeing anything. I took the gun from his hand, spun the cylinder to make sure it was loaded, then dragged him back into the shadows under the stairs and put the chair back where he had it. If anyone came checking on him they might think he only left his post for a minute and wouldn't be too worried.

Once past the guard I was able to get a better impression of the layout of the house. It rambled in all directions, doors opening into well-stocked pantries, linen closets and storage rooms. I had spotted two more men at critical points, but there was no way to move in on them without being seen. One gunshot would bring others running and I couldn't afford that.

Somewhere inside the house there was a burst of sound, voices laughing, muffled by the thickness of the walls. I stood in the niche of a doorway watching the man at the end of the corridor, saw him stretch, bored, then turn and walk in my direction. He got fifteen feet away, stopped, seemed to sense something, then shrugged and turned his back and returned to his original position.

Behind me the door I was leaning against opened with the faintest squeak. The guard stopped again, looked back over his shoulder, then decided to investigate and walked back. I had no choice except to step back through the door and close it, hoping he wouldn't notice the movement. His feet passed, then came by again as he satisfied himself that there was nobody there.

Now he'd be alert. I swore at myself for not jumping him when I could have, but it was too late now. I lit my last match, found myself in a kitchen cluttered with dirty dishes piled high on the sink, and an ancient gas range littered with used pots. Four rolling serving trays were lined against the wall next to a corridor that led somewhere into the bowels of the house.

The match flickered and went out, but I had my direction fixed and followed it in my mind.

And I found what I came for. Or at least some of it.

The two great sliding doors that opened onto the room were shut, but age had shrunk them so that a quarter-inch crack showed in their vertical alignment. I pressed my eye to the aperture to get a wider angle of vision and saw them, a small crowd, some in chairs, some standing smoking, enjoying the spectacle on the stage in the middle of the room.

A cage had been erected there about eight feet square, finger-thick bars covered with a thin wire mesh. She stood in the middle, absolutely motionless, uncomfortably poised on a small block of wood, her ink-black hair a startling contrast against the white negligee that had parted down the front and was thrown back over her shoulders. A false smile of frozen horror looked like it had been painted on her face, a look of total disbelief, yet somehow tinged with grim determination. Not a muscle in her body moved, and in the weird blue light that enveloped her I could see a reflection in her eyes as they followed the insidious motion of the two diamondback rattlesnakes that writhed restlessly just inches from her legs, their tongues nervous little feelers sensing danger in this strange atmosphere, their tails buzzing with anger.

I had found Greta Service again.

How long she had been there I couldn't tell, but the terrible agony of the position she was forced to hold was evident in the muscular tension of her legs. Any movement, no matter how slight, would bring those snakes striking to an attack.

A figure moved from behind a chair and I saw Belar Ris. For a second the light caught him and I could see his smile of enjoyment. He sat on the arm of the chair and draped his hand across the shoulder of the one sitting there.

From one side a voice said, "How long has it been, Belar?"

He looked at his watch. "Forty minutes."

Then the one in the chair said, "You're going to lose your bet, Belar. She's going to win your fifty thousand dollars."

My skin crawled all over because the answer was all right there in that room. *The voice was Dulcie McInnes'.*

And Belar Ris said, "No, I won't lose. You'll have your pleasure."

How long had you been doing it, Dulcie . . . finding the kind of woman who would submit to this kind of pleasure-seeking? You were in the right position for it. How many more were dead that we didn't know about? And how many ever did win the bet that they could outlast a distorted thirst for pleasure? And what was your gain, Dulcie . . . a greater social acceptance because of your associations? Who else did you entice into this tight circle who could be blackjacked

235

politically because he had become a blood brother to depravity?

It must have shaken her when I came into the picture because until then it all would have been so carefully planned and executed. They had the money and the means to operate with and always the knowledge that the shield of diplomatic immunity was there for them.

What was your shield, Dulcie? Or was money and power satisfaction enough?

I could see more of the faces now. They were the faces of those from countries of sudden wealth and emergence into power, but who still reveled in the savageries of the near-primitive. But not all. Several I had seen at the Flamingo Room the other night enjoying their respectability.

Dulcie's choice of subjects had been excellent. They were women alone with no one to care about them. They would do anything for a chance at a small fortune.

The exception had been Greta who did have somebody who cared about her. She was willing to take the big gamble because she cared about somebody too. Harry Service might not have been worth it, but he was all she had and she was going to keep her promise to him.

Her face was tighter now than before, fighting the unbearable strain of her position and the proximity of the snakes.

Too bad Mitch Temple couldn't see what he had stumbled upon. He started chasing down a murderer because a single thread seemed to tie in the deaths of two girls, two inexpensive, sexy nylon negligees. He did the legwork in countless shops and was lucky enough to spot Belar Ris buying another one. Even when he published Belar Ris's activities in his column, he might not have made any personal contact with the man, so he verified his identification by going through the morgue files until he located Ris's picture.

Even his call to Norm Harrison fitted in. You couldn't openly accuse a man in his position unless you had positive proof. But Norm had been out of town. Mitch did have another source of information going for him. Ronald Miller probably had told him about his company's litigation with Belar Ris in the theft of the C-130. That fitted in too. Ali Duval could have seen the shipment, recognized its potential to Ris and gotten it ashore.

Mitch's trouble was, Ronald Miller had left too and Mitch had no place to go to except the source itself. It would be like him to call Ris, ostensibly to arrange for an interview on some matter or other, then try to draw him out. But Ris had something going for him too. Mitch's picture was at the top of his column. Ris could have recognized Mitch and seen through the whole skein and stopped it right there with a single knife thrust through Mitch's heart.

Yet it *didn't* stop there. I was looking for Greta and Greta could have led me to them if I pushed hard enough. She had already been recruited and was ready for them regardless of what happened to the other girls who went ahead of her. She had probably been held right here for this very night and she was doing it of her own volition.

They didn't know what I had though. The papers had made a big thing of my reputation and they couldn't take a chance. Orslo Bucher was one of their own nationals and could be called upon for the small jobs. He searched my place, then tried for me and died doing it. That threw it back at them again.

I still kept looking for Greta.

So they let Greta come to me.

Ali Duval arranged to use Virginia Howell's room through Lorenzo Jones, a far-out contact that could have no possible connection with anyone. It was a simple thing for Dulcie to drop a card into Teddy Gates' rotary file and lead me to it, and just as simple to remove it again and send Gates off on an appointment that would lead to his death. The red herrings and the wild geese were all over the place to foul up the trail.

The thing they didn't plan for was Lorenzo Jones' curiosity about Ali. Jones could smell a buck and would chase it, but he could smell trouble too and was scared to death of it. They didn't plan on me pushing it any further after I had seen Greta. She was there because she wanted to be there. She had to be there if she wanted the chance at the big stakes she coveted so desperately.

Dulcie, you damn fool. It couldn't last. You couldn't keep it covered forever.

There was a hum of voices, then a cold hush. I looked through the crack again. Greta had tottered on the block and both the snakes were poised, tongues flicking to find the source of movement, their buttons a steady, sharp buzz in the quiet.

It had to be now.

I jammed the two guns in my belt, felt for the handles that were indented into the frames of the doors and got my feet braced. I was ready to tear them apart when I heard the shouting and saw a tall guy run in from an alcove and point behind him.

"The dog. It has been killed. Someone is inside."

The one in front of the door was too intent on what the other had said and didn't hear me until I was almost through the opening. He whirled, struck out at me and caught the side of the .45 across his face and went down with a scream.

Confusion was immediate. They tried to run and had no place to go. There were more of them than I expected, but they had no way of knowing how many were coming behind me and their first thought was to get out. They were there for pleasure and stayed for panic and when the guy at the door blasted two quick shots in my direction it added to the turmoil. The crowd parted in front of me, faces and bodies just a blur in the dim light.

Not Greta though. She never moved. She couldn't.

I let go two quick blasts through the cage and took the heads off the snakes just as she let herself go and crumpled up on top of their thrashing bodies.

They came in fast from all sides, gun muzzles winking death, the roar lost in the screams and hoarse shouts of the ones trying to get away. I caught one in the chest and shot the leg out from under another, but they weren't the ones I wanted.

Belar Ris was my target and he was someplace in the dark.

I almost had it made. I took down one who blocked the exit and I almost made the door. I could have brought those agents patrolling the area swarming onto the place with a couple of fast gunshots into the night and they could have taken over and finished the job.

That *almost* was the big one. My luck ran out. I felt the searing finger crease my skull and I went down on my face, hoping the blackness would come before the pain.

The lolling motion of my head woke me up. Dizzy waves of pain swept over me and my stomach heaved in the spasms of nausea. I felt twisted out of shape and tried to pull myself together but couldn't move. My feet were tied and my hands bound together behind my back. I forced my eyes open, saw the two who carried me, and beside the ones who held me under the arms, Dulcie and Belar Ris.

Dog met dog again. He saw me looking at him

and said, "You are a fool."

But I didn't answer him. I looked at the other dog and said to Dulcie, "Hello, bitch."

She didn't answer me. The one carrying my feet stopped and said, "In here, Belar?"

"Yes, with the others, Ali."

He let my feet go and turned, taking a set of keys from his pocket. This time I got a good look at his face. I had seen it twice before. Once in a news photo standing near Belar Ris. But the first time was when I was leaving Dulcie's office and he stepped out of the elevator.

The picture was complete. Only no one was going to see it. Like the one Cleo painted of me, I thought. That was all that was left. My eyes closed and I felt my head fall again, but I could still hear them.

Dulcie said, "You think it's safe?"

Belar's voice was a deep rumble. "The windows are barred and the door is triple locked. They'll keep until we can dispose of them."

"But . . ."

He cut her short. "You get upstairs and quiet the others. Someone could have heard the shooting. If there's an inquiry we can arrange to have the guards say there was a prowler on the grounds. If not, we'll simply sit down, let everyone return to normal and discuss how we can get rid of the bodies this one provided us with."

I heard the door swing open, then I was tossed inside and the door closed with a metallic clang behind me and the bolts shot home. I lay there waiting, retching at the pain that was like a hot iron against my head, the cold concrete of the floor grinding against my face.

Then there was the rasp of a match and a light blossomed in the corner of the room and a familiar voice said, "Mike?"

Surprise shook me back to normal. I saw her face in the light, grimy with dirt, but smiling. "Hi, Velda." You'd think we were meeting for lunch.

She laughed, reached up and pulled a cord. A single bulb suspended from the ceiling came on, the light barely reaching the corners of the room. She came over, untied my hands and feet, watched while I rubbed the circulation back into them and looked at the cut on my scalp. It was superficial, but painful. At least I wouldn't die from it.

When I could stand up she pointed behind me. Greta Service was lying there, hands and feet tied, a large, blue bruise on her forehead. "They brought her here first," Velda said. "Are there any others?"

"No."

She bent down and untied Greta, then massaged her into gradual consciousness. I let her get done, made sure Greta was all right, then pulled Velda up to me. "Let's have it, kitten. How the hell did you get here?"

"Julie Pelham. That man found her. He must have been looking for her and forced her into the car, then didn't know what to do with her. I saw them go by, grabbed the plate number and had it checked out. It was registered to one of the ones in the legation that occupies this building. I tried to come in through a back way, got cornered by one of those dogs and a guard grabbed me. They were having a conference on what to do with me when some of the others began arriving, so they tied me up and dumped me in here. It took me about an hour to break loose, but at least I wasn't shut up in the dark."

"What happened to the girl?"

Velda pointed toward the far corner with her thumb. "Look."

Two bodies were curled together in a heap. "They both made mistakes," I said. "He couldn't explain the girl, but she explained him." I glanced around me peering into the shadows. "Have you checked this place out?"

"It's part of an old laundry. Those are washtubs down there and there's an old gas stove that leaks. That one window leads out to the ground level. I think we're in the back of the house somewhere, but I'm not sure. The window bars go right into the cement."

She tried to sound matter-of-fact about it, but I could feel the rising fear in her inflection. "Take it easy, kid. Let me look around."

There was no chance of going through the door. It was too heavy and too securely bolted. The only other way out was the window. The glass was on the other side of the bars, coated with black paint. I felt the bars themselves, inch-thick pieces of metal with only a surface coating of rust. At a first glance they seemed to be an impregnable barrier, but the iron had feet of clay.

The old cement they were imbedded in had been eroded by dampness and leakage and I could scratch a groove in it with my fingernail. I went over to the old stove, pulled off one of the grates and began chipping away. It powdered at first, then the cracks appeared and I pulled it loose by chunks. In ten minutes I had the bars wrenched out of place. I didn't have a gun any more, but those bars would make a good weapon if we needed one.

Greta moaned and sat up, one hand going to her head. She was still only half conscious and unaware of what was going on. I got my arms around her to pull her to her feet when I heard a short muffled buzz and held up my hand for Velda to be quiet. After a few seconds it came again, then once more and was cut off in the middle. I let Greta go and went over to the cabinet beside the stove. I pulled the door open.

Inside on the shelf was an old phone buried under a heap of moldy towels. I picked the receiver up gently, but whoever was on the other end was just hanging up. I held the hook down, let it go and listened but there was no dial tone.

The expectant look on Velda's face disappeared when I shook my head. "It rings on an incoming call, but you can't call out. It's an old model they forgot to disengage when they installed the new ones. It only works because there's a crossed wire somewhere."

"But if someone calls in . . . we could tell them . . ." She stopped, realizing the improbability of it.

Yet . . . *something* could be done with that phone. We might not make it out of the grounds, but we could leave our fist behind us. I pulled it out as far as I could, pried the guts out of it so that only the ringing mechanism was left. I unscrewed the bells and tied a nail to the clapper with a shoelace for greater leverage. Then I fastened the crazy rig to the light bulb so that when the phone rang that bulb was going to be smashed to bits.

Velda watched me, but I didn't take the time to explain it to her. When I was through I went to the window, swung it outward on its hinges and helped Velda climb through. She and I both managed to get Greta out and when they were ready I went back, pulled the burners off the stove so the gas would come through at full pressure and climbed out the window. When I pushed it back in place I picked up the iron bars, handed one to Velda and said, "Let's go."

And the lady with the luck smiled on us. This time she was giving us a free roll of the dice. The night was our friend and the shadows our love. The guards were still there, but their anxiety made them too alert and they exposed themselves so we were able to skirt around their positions. The cool wind was at our backs so no scent reached the dogs and we made the wall and found a way over it.

The car wasn't too far away, still concealed where I had hidden it and we got in and I started up and pulled out on the dirt road. A quarter mile down other cars paraded in their vigil, protecting those behind the walls from those outside.

It was the wrong way around, I thought.

We passed through Bradbury, found an open gas station and went in and cleaned up. I looked at the clock. In a little while the sun would be coming up.

I used one of George's credit cards he kept in the glove compartment to wangle some cash out of the station attendant. He figured us for Saturday-night drunks and had that happen to him before and the tip was worth his handing me the change.

I made one call to Hy from the pay station outside and told him to get me the number of the phone in the building Belar Ris' group occupied. Hy called back in five minutes, but I wouldn't give him any information. I said I'd tell him later and I would. It was a shame he'd never be able to print it.

Velda and Greta Service came out and got in the car. I was dropping a dime in the slot when a city patrol car drove up and a uniformed cop got out, fishing in his pocket for some change. He saw me in the booth and stood outside waiting patiently while I dialed.

By now that single room would be gas-packed, a monstrous potential of destruction waiting to be triggered into instant hell.

In my ear I heard the stutter of the ringing phone.

Six miles away a brilliant glow of orange blossomed like a night flower into the sky, lasted seconds at its apex and died with the speed of its blooming. There were more seconds of night-quiet, then the thunderous roar came in with its wave of shock that rattled the windows in the buildings behind us.

The cop's mouth dropped open, his face still taut with surprise. "What the hell was that!"

"Wrong number," I said and walked to the car.